In the Cards
A Global Epic of the Heart

*For Aunt Edith,
Love you to the Moon
and back!*

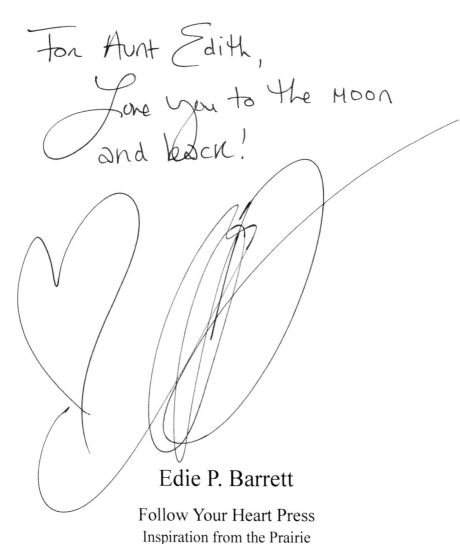

Edie P. Barrett

Follow Your Heart Press
Inspiration from the Prairie

In the Cards: A Global Epic of the Heart
Copyright ©2018 by Edie Barrett.
ISBN: 978-1-5323-7377-0

All rights reserved. No portion of this book may be reproduced, stored in a retrieval system, or transmitted in any form or by any means— electronic, mechanical, photocopy, recording, scanning, or other— except for brief quotations in critical reviews or articles, without the prior written permission of the publisher.

This novel is a work of fiction with some elements of truth. Other than the father, all characters are fictional and are a product of the author's imagination. Other than a photograph the author has, all aspects of the lover are fictional. Any resemblance to real life counterparts is coincidental. There are exceptions: a quote and a reference to Richard Tarnas. This quote and his name were used with his permission. There are also references to the work of Joseph Campbell and James Hillman.

Cover Design: Corina Kells of Dawson, Minnesota
                  Corina Kells Art and Photography, LLC

Author Photograph: Caiti Barr, Ortonville, Minnesota

Editor: Cathy Bernardi Jones, Waseca, Minnesota

Production Editor: Joy Minion
                  Minion Editing & Design, Moorhead, Minnesota

Published by Follow Your Heart Press, Ortonville, Minnesota

Printed in Fergus Falls, Minnesota

In 2017, Edie Barrett received a grant to support this creative writing project. This activity is made possible by a grant from the Southwest Minnesota Arts Council with funds appropriated by the McKnight Foundation.

"There comes a point in your life
when you need to stop reading
other people's books and write your own."

Albert Einstein

Acknowledgments

Although I have been creative my entire life, my commitment to Jungian psychology, which began around 1996, shifted my work both as a fine artist and as a writer.

My Jungian journey began through employment. I was the program administrator for the Department of Mythological Studies at Pacifica Graduate Institute in Santa Barbara, California. The chair, Dr. Mahaffey, and I ran the department together for more than thirteen years. Pacifica is a world-renowned private graduate school of Jungian and depth psychology.

When I think of Pacifica, I first need to acknowledge Stephen Aizenstat, founder and past president. He is truly a global visionary. The graduate school that he created is remarkable, and I was grateful to be part of it.

I had an extraordinary supervisor. Patrick Mahaffey is one of the most honorable and enlightened people I have met in my life. I will always treasure the years that we worked together and take pride in the quality of department that we strived to cultivate. Our friendship remains deeply meaningful to me.

I was surrounded by stellar academics. Most are known internationally for their work. I need to single out Dennis Slattery, who has a great passion for classical literature and for teaching the work of Joseph Campbell. *The Hero's Journey* is one of Campbell's works that Slattery taught at Pacifica. I credit him for my inspiration in wanting to showcase Campbell's work in this novel. In addition, Dennis Slattery gave a fantastic graduation address at Pacifica titled, "The Mythic Journey to One's Self." Slattery's graduation address inspired my own personal spin on the hero's story and Emma's graduation address that you will find in this novel. Dennis is an avid writer and possesses a genuine investment in other people's success. His generosity is symbolic of the way he lives his life. I am deeply grateful for our continuing friendship. Many blessings to you, Dennis!

Other people in the department during my time there included Christine Downing and David Miller, who are both revered academics and professionals. I absolutely loved working with them. There is the thoughtful Glen Slater, whose presence is reflective and grounded. Hendrika de Vries taught personal mythology and possesses a delightful laugh. She embodies it all: the beauty of the feminine and the wisdom of the crone. I would like to acknowledge the late Walter Odajnyk, whom I deeply respected and appreciated as a friend. Next is Ginette Paris, who has a beautiful French Montréal accent, is a fashion palette, and delivered articulate lectures with everyone spellbound. Kathleen Jenks stepped right out of a fairy tale and was enchanting to work with. I appreciated the deep integrity of Zaman Stanizai, the utterly charming Evans Lansing Smith, and the perspectives of Lionel Corbett. Laura Grillo, from Chicago, shared her deep love of African traditions and academic excellence. I would also like to acknowledge the late Daniel Noel. I enjoyed working with him very much.

I attended as many conferences as I could over the years at Pacifica. A number of presentations stand out in my mind as influential: Richard Tarnas is at the top of that list. You will find my character Parker honoring his work. I always enjoyed being in the presence of Richard Tarnas and always came away richer for it. My character Parker uses a direct quote from Tarnas' book, *The Passion of the Western Mind*. I have a great respect for the way Richard thinks and writes. I appreciate him allowing me to reproduce this quote in this novel. Thank you Richard!

Also at the top of the list is Marion Woodman. Just as this book was about to go to press, she passed away. I will treasure the personal relationship I had with her the rest of my life. She was keenly observant of human behavior, direct, and honest. She had a feminine perspective which was anchored in the body; this was her significant contribution to Jungian psychology. She was an old-fashioned letter writer. I have a collection of handwritten letters from her, acquired over our years of friendship. These letters are sacred to me. From this vast, open, beautiful prairie, I put my hands together and blow her one thousand kisses.

James Hillman: I will never forget someone running around campus trying to find me because Hillman was on the phone and wanted to talk to me. When I picked up the phone, he wanted to know whom I thought should edit his next book, "because I knew everyone." Of course, who wouldn't stand up a bit straighter after that! I also treasure the memory of sitting next to him at a departmental dinner at a fancy restaurant. We innocently flirted with each other throughout the meal and then shared a slice of lemon tart. More than once I heard him referred to as the Mick Jagger of the Jungian world. True enough. We lost Hillman in 2011.

I was profoundly grateful to meet Robert A. Johnson. I honor his perspective: simple, accessible, and relatable. I have purchased *Balancing Heaven and Earth* more than any other book to give as a gift. It is a great place to begin with Jungian psychology.

I need to acknowledge a weekend conference with Maladoma Somé. He is a West African elder and is a world-renowned author and teacher. His work on honoring our ancestors through ritual changed my life and helped me to appreciate the larger intention for telling this story.

Other inspirational people whom I want to mention are Kathleen Berry, Jean Shinoda Bolen, Phil Cousineau, Cathy Diorio, Nancy Galindo, James Hollis, Leslie Kent Kunkel, Sally MacColl, Linda Schierse Leonard, Monica McCarthy, the late Stephen Marcus, Diane Norcross, my favorite sociology professor at UCSB, the late Tamotsu Shibutani, and Mary Watkins.

I worked with nearly one thousand MA and PhD students. Pacifica attracted students from all over the world, and they arrived inspired. Obviously, there are too many to mention, but I need to name one: Hea Kyoung Koh, a South Korean student. She embodies both generosity and grace. Her dissertation focused on Cheju Island, Korea, and her research inspired me to write about that location. Because it is an island off the mainland, it has a distinctive culture. Historically, women had careers as divers, which resulted in economic power and nontraditional gender roles. The island culture has had a deep reverence for the snakes that reside there; they are treated as sacred creatures. I have tried to honor Hea Kyoung's research and perspective of Cheju. Thank you Hea Kyoung! Thank you for your beautiful friendship and support of my creative work. I trust that our paths will cross again.

During my twenty-six years in Santa Barbara, I was part of a small women's group who met for eleven years. That group consisted of Dianne Skafte, Maureen Murdock, and Ginette Paris. What an amazing blessing to be with these women in an intimate circle. My love and respect for them is simply off the charts.

I also want to acknowledge Lawrence Hillman and his innovative work on leadership. He is currently collaborating with Richard Olivier (out of London) and conducting workshops on business and leadership through an archetypal lens. I flew to St. Louis in 2017 to attend one of their workshops. It was an illuminating experience in so many ways!

I would be remiss not to name Mary Kay Holland, for her incredible wisdom and gifted insight.

Living on the rural prairie, I am very grateful for the inspiration I receive from *On Being*, Krista Tippett's amazing podcasts (Minnesota Public Radio). I also have a deep appreciation for The Asheville Jung Center and its webinar offerings.

Simply put, my creative life is enriched by psychological perspectives and self-understanding. This novel would never have happened without the influence of these people, their work, and my commitment to a personal psychological journey.

Speaking of which, I need to acknowledge my therapist in Santa Barbara, Dr. Teague. He was able to beautifully hold the alchemical cauldron for me to transform my life and embrace my creative journey. I offer a deep bow of reverence to him.

I have been working with a personal coach over the last three years, Pam Fuhrman, whom I met at Pacifica. I have found her support incredibly valuable. While I tend to be fairly goal oriented, being accountable to her has really kept me on track. In addition, I am so grateful to have her as a faithful companion on this creative journey. Thank you so much, Pam. You are an unexpected blessing in my life!

I would like to thank the dream analysis group here in Ortonville, Minnesota, which has been meeting since 2011: John and Lila Salls, Neva Foster, Deb Larson, Stephanie Pelowski, Hisa Kilde, Mark Mustful, Vicky Radel, and Janet Rois.

I would also like to thank the women's support group that I am part of here on the prairie: Audrey Arner, Athena Kildegaard, Kathryn Draeger, Lauren Carlson, Marianne Zarzana, Vicky Radel, Lucy Tokheim, and Julie Stevens.

Southwest Minnesota Arts Council needs to be acknowledged for its support of my work, both as an artist and a writer. I have been tremendously grateful for the grants that I have been awarded. For many years, Greta Murray, as executive director, was a fantastic asset to our region for her commitment to the arts. With Greta's retirement, Nicole DeBoer is at the helm. I am so grateful for her support and guidance. *Thank you, Nicole!*

Because the arts are such an important part of my life, I would like to acknowledge the following people for their committed vision to honoring and supporting me and the arts in our region: Deb Larson, for her genuine investment in my creative process. Whether it's helping me set-up for an exhibit, or telling me about art opportunities, or simply reading my work. Deb, you are an absolute blessing and treasure in my life! Thank you! I would also like to acknowledge Becky Parker and Liz Rackl for their friendship, vision and support of the arts in our region. Their dedication, work and support of the arts is impressive.

I have a great editor! Her name is Cathy Bernardy Jones. I appreciate her keen, observant eye. Cathy, your investment in this story and your suggestions have been incredibly valuable to me. Thank you!

Joy Minion is my Production Editor. I think of her as being my novel's midwife. Her skill set is a very unique niche and I am grateful for her contributions to my work.

The cover of this book was designed by my niece, Corina Kells. Thank you Corina for sharing your talents with me! I love you so much! This particular set of cards was given to me by a friend who purchased it in an antique shop in Denver. It dates back to the late 1800s and was produced by a card company out of France called B. P. Grimaud.

I would be remiss not to acknowledge two very long-term friendships. I need to thank my childhood friend Jesslyn Brown. We have been friends for nearly fifty years. At this point, she is more like a family member then a girlfriend. I love you so much Jess! Another friend that

I would like to mention is Kathy Ansite, who remains my dear friend from our undergraduate days at UCSB. I am so grateful we have shared over thirty years together. Thank you Kathy! I love you!

It is important I acknowledge my sister, Kathleen Marihart, for being a lifelong friend and supporter of my creative work. I am so deeply grateful that you and I share this journey of life together. "Thank you" falls profoundly short of my gratitude. I love you to the moon and back! I would like to acknowledge my little half-sister, Tifney LaCabe. Because she grew up with our father, her support and encouragement on this project has been monumental to me. Thank you so much Tifney! I love you! To Tanya Reed, my cousin and dear friend, I send you love and abundant blessings.

In the summer of 2012 I hosted Jiayi ("Winnie") Wu from Cheng-du, the capital of Sichuan, China. She spent her junior year in high school here in Ortonville. She has returned twice. Winnie graduated in 2017 from Oklahoma State University with a degree in accounting and hopes to attend graduate school in Seattle.

In 2016 I hosted Tan Liya ("Leah") from Hefei, in the eastern province of Anhui, China. She was here on behalf of the National Committee on U.S. China Relations. Leah participated in a Professional Fellows Program administrated by the National Committee on behalf of the U.S. Department of State. She was here to explore environmental awareness and protection. Her host organization was CURE of Montevideo. Leah returned to Ortonville June 2017 for a visit.

xvi

By opening both my home and my heart to these two beautiful women, the world became a little smaller, a little more connected and my life certainly became richer. I consider Winnie to be my Chinese "daughter" and Leah to be my very precious Chinese friend. Both Winnie and Leah have been a tremendous blessing to me.

I would like to thank my mother, who always believed in my talent and ability. Anything that I wanted to do, she believed was attainable. As a daughter, this was a tremendous gift. It is also important to acknowledge my grandmother, Edith Kamp, and my aunt, Kathleen Kamp, and all of the years we sat around the table drinking tea and reading tea leaves. I would also like to thank my aunt, Edith Fraser, who resides in Sandiway, England. You have been a treasure throughout my entire life, and I love you dearly.

Of course, I need to thank my father for providing me with the story that inspired the film script and subsequent novel. Once upon a time he loved a Korean woman. There are some bread crumbs of truth scattered throughout the story, but nearly all of it reflects my imaginal and creative process. It is my hope that my work honors him and the Korean woman he loved so long ago.

And last, but not least, I offer my deep gratitude to you, dear reader. I hope that you enjoy this book. I wish you all the best on your own self-understanding, creative journey and path of love.

Edie Barrett

The unspoken result of war
and international peace efforts
are thousands of orphans
fathered by soldiers serving in the military.

This novel is dedicated
to the women and children all over the
world who were loved and left behind
in the mission of peace.

Randall J. Lawrence
January 8, 1992
Looking Back on August 15, 1953
Teague, Korea

    Saying good-bye took longer than I had planned. An unvoiced premonition lived between In-sook and I. It had for some time. Any words or gestures I made would have rightfully been deemed invalid. She knew I wouldn't be back anytime soon, even with the best of intentions.
    Outside, my driver impatiently honked the Jeep horn for the third time. In-sook, so flawlessly exquisite, was the most beautiful woman I had ever seen. She calmly stood in the doorway, with her left hand resting on her pregnant stomach, her gold wedding ring reflecting the sunlight.
    At the time it didn't seem reasonable to bring her back to the States. I couldn't return home with a Korean woman, especially a pregnant one. Rural Minnesota was no place for us in the 1950's. Although my parents were good people, it would have been more than their Norwegian heritage could bear. I loved her, but I was also young, naive, and full of bravado. I thought love grew on trees and that my life would provide me one abundant harvest after another.
    After leaving Korea, I spent years—decades—searching for the quality of love that In-sook and I had shared. I looked for women to fill the void she had

effortlessly filled. I had more children, always seeking to rectify my previous shortcoming. The truth is, I had fallen deeply in love with a woman from another culture but had lacked the moral strength to honor her in America.

For years I was haunted by a recurring nightmare: I was drowning in a lake, surrounded by life rafts that deflated whenever I reached to grasp them. In-sook knelt on a nearby dock, her hand outstretched to save me.

I was an old man when I finally found the courage to swim to the dock and take her extended hand.

Amber Nelson
July 9, 2005
Santa Barbara, California

♦

I am here to do card readings for Emma's birthday party. I learned to read cards from my eccentric Aunt Minnie, who was taught the art by Russian gypsies while visiting St. Petersburg in the early 1960's. My casual introduction turned into a lifelong passion to understand the divine, the sacred unseen world. My interest, of course, needed to be grounded academically. My parents' anxiety began to soar as they imagined their only daughter in the back of a caravan, traveling the country roads of Romania reading fortunes.

To appease them and to satisfy my own educational desires, I earned my PhD in cultural archeology and wrote my dissertation on divination. Since then, I've traveled the world, thrown bones with the Africans, read tea leaves with the British, and tossed coins with the Chinese.

My sun is in Sagittarius and my moon in Scorpio. In other words, I'm quite outgoing but have a deep and profound emotional side. My birth numbers add up to eight. Translated, this means my life will be very karmic. I have the gift to influence people and events, and I must always use my innate wisdom responsibly and ethically.

I've become quite famous for my skills. I've published two successful books and have been interviewed on television a few times. I'm frequently invited to lecture at international conferences. That's the funny thing about fortune-telling: people are fascinated, whether they believe or not. How can they resist? Fortune-telling dates back to the early origins of man. Imagine the images of Shamans in the caves of France. The deep psyche of the earth holds the remnants of our history, our desire to commune with our ancestors, our longing to understand forces greater than ourselves.

I live in England during the summer, in Ross-on-Wye, a beautiful, quaint village with cobblestones and a river that runs through the heart of town. I spend winters in Santa Barbara, home of my alma mater.

While promoting my recent book here in Santa Barbara, I did a reading and book signing at Chelsie's Bookstore. Chelsie's Bookstore has managed to survive Amazon.com, and it's as if the whole city has agreed to support this historical treasure. A woman about my age (in splendid yoga shape, I might add), wearing a Buddha T-shirt, lingered by the display table while looking at me nervously. Her T-shirt had a glimmering rhinestone smack-dab in the third eye of the Buddha. Being an "eight" woman, I know my chakras. It was that Buddha T-shirt that made me say "yes."

I should have known better, but who am I to question destiny and my place in its plan? I know this kind of woman. She emerges in every city. She wants to ask a personal question, or she has a loved one to inquire after. She's a pilgrim searching for answers to the mysteries of her life. I am empathetic, for I too, am a pilgrim.

4

It was well past closing time; only five of us remained in the bookstore. The manager locked the door, his keys clanging against the metal door frame in a less-than-subtle hint. Realizing there was limited time, Buddha woman came forward and introduced herself as Roxanne. She bought a copy of my book and asked me to sign it. I prepared for a litany of questions, but they didn't materialize. Instead, Roxanne asked me to attend a small, intimate birthday party for her friend Emma. I would be the "Oracle for Hire."

I don't do parties. I am not a clown act. I don't tie balloons or jump out of a cake. This request made me want to stand up, brush the creases out of my skirt, and reintroduce myself as Dr. Nelson. Instead, I sat there, thinking. There are 150 ways to say no. I began to select one from my repertoire, but meanwhile Buddha peacefully watched me from inside the lotus blossom, the facets of his rhinestone shining into my third eye.

"Yes," I heard myself say.

Good god. Where did that come from?

Roxanne was thrilled. She then proceeded to tell me about her friend Emma: her dedication to her high school English students, her work with wounded birds, her generosity as a friend.

"I would be delighted." There it was again. This voice—my voice—agreeing, *consenting.*

Although I read cards for my friends and family on a regular basis, it has been years since I walked into a room to do readings with unknown people. I steer clear of the "surprise gift." What may be a great idea for Roxanne might not be so for Emma. It's best if people choose

5

divination for themselves. I have learned this, sometimes the hard way.

It was that Buddha T-shirt that persuaded me. Buddha: an icon of enlightenment, truth, wisdom, and deep inner peace. I have a Buddha head that sits on my coffee table. I keep a small Japanese *ikebana* floral arrangement next to him. It is a personal shrine that visually reminds me of breathing, of balance, of kindness and peaceful grace. Buddha was the oracle who brought me to Emma.

That's the way of oracles. Oracles are road signs from the divine. They inform us of our path in a world cluttered with distractions. They come in unexpected messengers, through nature, through image and word. Like the Buddha T-shirt. Why did Roxanne wear that shirt on that particular night? Chances are she has a closet full of other options. Little did she know it would have such meaning for me. Buddha's image, with the rhinestone third eye, reminded me of my obligation to others, an obligation infused with generosity and kindness. I trust oracles; they guide my life. The divine sees the "big picture" of our lives, while we earthbound creatures put one foot in front of the other, often oblivious to our larger story.

All of this leads me to this moment. I am dressed beautifully. I've worked hard to dispel the stereotype of a psychic. We can all conjure up images of the wild, untamed hair, the long, gauzy skirts and hoop earrings. I am never what people expect. My clothes are classically simple and clearly expensive. Tonight I wear an ornate necklace of chunk amethyst. Amethyst is associated with the crown chakra, with Buddha. When my grandmother was dying at 103 years old, I performed a death ritual for her. She wore this same necklace. It looked so beautiful on her. She was a queen prepared to meet her destiny, adorned with gems at the threshold. This necklace is powerful. I knew it would be appropriate for this evening. On some critical level, when I chose this necklace, it prepared me for Emma.

Roxanne opens her front door beaming, clearly excited about my arrival. Roxanne has great energy, with or without her Buddha T-shirt. She radiates clarity, good health, and a blueblood, ivy-league education. She gestures for me to come in. I step into her living room and quickly survey my surroundings. Roxanne's home is simple and tasteful, with contemporary art on the walls. There's not a speck of clutter, and I imagine she arranges her clothes by season and color. I like her house because it reflects her. It has good feng shui. I know this term is now passé, but any belief system that has lasted more than three thousand years has done so for good reason.

Two women are seated on the fluffy pillowed couch. A good-sized coffee table anchors the living room. Plates with remnants of abandoned chocolate cake are set to one side. Emma's birthday gifts have already been opened. Creased gift wrap lies folded with a pile of satin ribbon on top. My timing is perfect. Although we are in the middle of summer, it has been a foggy, cool day. A gentle fire burns in the fireplace, adding warmth to the already inviting ambiance.

Enthusiastically, Roxanne invites me to sit on a chair next to the couch, then proceeds to introduce me to her friends Savannah and Emma. Savannah is African American. Her hair is a maze of cornrow braids with small charms woven into the braids themselves. Her look exudes creativity and humor. California will forever be safe from any energy shortage with a smile like hers. She has an endearing Southern drawl that drips of deep-fried chicken and grits. I instantly adore her. She is surely the pride and joy of her parents, aunts and uncles, and cousins twice removed. Sometimes I don't need cards or coins or palms to "see" a person's karma. With no information, I have her number, and it's a good one.

Then there's Emma, the birthday guest of honor. She dresses conservatively, a classic beauty with smooth, flawless skin. Her long brown hair cascades over her shoulders. At forty-four, she has a reserved demeanor and watches me like a hawk. I sense she is already working hard to inoculate herself against any insight I might offer. I can tell she is a skeptic and new to divination.

I have brought the tools of my art: a selection of cards, sacred candle, and matches. All are carefully packed into an ornate traveling case I purchased in Venice. The three women form a captivated audience, and there's an anxious nervousness in the air as I begin to speak. "There are countless forms of divination. This method of card reading, which uses a traditional deck of cards, is called cartomancy. It dates back to at least the 1600s. Historically, cards were used only for divination." I pause to look at the women before resuming. "I've found that the cards are highly reliable for information, but even the Pythoness of Delphi could not always be a perfect channel. The entrance to the Oracle at Delphi bears the words, 'Know Thyself.' Remember, you always have free will to choose what is right for you."

I look at each of the women in turn. "Have you thought of the questions you would like to ask?" Emma appears anxious, Savannah sparkles with anticipation, and Roxanne meets my gaze without reservation.

Roxanne is the first to offer a question. "I have a job promotion I'm considering. I'd like to ask about that." This is a perfect question for a diviner, and I'm pleased.

I turn next to Savannah. A smile consumes her entire face. "I want to ask about romance!" she says, with her eyes flashing at me. I can't help but smile back at her. Romance questions can be tricky; clearly she hopes for a specific and positive outcome.

I turn to Emma; my eyes meet hers. She looks at me blankly, as if she has just stepped off a plane in some foreign land and doesn't speak the language. She responds nervously, "I don't know what to ask. I've never done anything like this before."

I do my best to coach her with a question: "What about your job? Perhaps you have a pending trip? Family questions are also appropriate."

Emma is completely stumped. "Do I have to have a specific question? Couldn't you just read the cards to see what they say?" she asks.

This is often a naive strategy used to remain anonymous. I look at her to assess the depth of her character. Of course, a general question *is* an option. Although for a beginner, there can be some advantage to focusing the inquiry—corralling the energy. An open question can lift the lid off Pandora's Box. Truth has a way of galloping forward like a herd of stallions finally freed.

My silence does not deter Emma. With new confidence she looks me in the eye and says, "Yes, I think a general reading would be good."

"All right then, since we're all here to celebrate you, why don't you go first?"

"Okay," Emma says with a bit of reservation.

From my Italian case, I take the candle, matches, and the selection of cards and lay them on the coffee table. "When we open the oracular circle, I always begin with a silent meditation. I believe this helps to put all of us—including myself—in a place of being present and receptive."

I light the candle, lean back into the chair, and close my eyes.

For me, this is how I honor my ancestors and my guides for their presence and for the work we are about to engage. Although most Christians would define it as an oxymoron, it is how I humble myself in the presence of God. I silently ask for a blessing on all who are here, especially Emma, who is celebrating her birthday. I ask for clarity, vision, and articulation of the message. I acknowledge that what is revealed to us this evening is in our highest good.

There is something about opening with a meditation and silent prayer, beginning the ritual of divination with a sense of respect and gratitude that sets the tone. This small gesture moves me out of myself and away from my own ego.

I open my eyes and watch the other women, one at a time, open theirs. Excited glances are exchanged.

I begin to lay out a selection of eight decks of cards onto the coffee table. Each deck rests in a gold mesh bag. Each has a king or queen who peers through the veil as if beckoning the time traveler. I've collected cards in my travels across the world. Each deck has a story, and each has a symbolic mood that infuses the reading. For me, divination begins when a deck is selected.

Emma points to the deck of the "Old Souls." This is a Viennese deck, and the face cards are exquisite. I remove the other cards from the coffee table and open the golden bag she has chosen. I look at Emma, already aware this reading will encompass other lifetimes and future karmic issues. I pass the cards to her. "Shuffle the cards as much as you like. Return them to me when you feel they are ready."

Emma's hands carefully shuffle her fate. Everyone is quiet. Emma gives the cards to me. I select each card that lies under a seven, and lay out the following: eight of clubs, ten of clubs, queen of diamonds, ace of hearts, joker, five of spades, three of diamonds, and three of spades. I spread the remaining cards on the table face-side down. "Please take any three cards," I say to Emma.

Emma selects the ten of spades, king of spades (upside down), and jack of hearts.

I remove the remainder of the deck from the table.

I sit before the spread of cards, navigating destiny, star gazing. I'm analyzing the constellations from this point in time, from this chair in Roxanne's home, and from Emma herself. I'm a pilot in the utter darkness of an African night with nothing but the vast expanse of the universe above me, the solitude of the silent land beneath me, and my own internal compass.

I take a deep breath and begin. "Emma, you are represented by the queen of diamonds. You are a very old soul. The spirit world rejoices in who you are and the power and gifts you bring to the world. Beauty defines you. You have an exquisite home. It is a sanctuary for you, and you find it rejuvenating to be there. You have a deep appreciation for arts and culture. These things are actually quite significant in contributing to your health and happiness. It is important that you understand this."

Roxanne and Savannah smile at each other. Emma relaxes, hearing from me what she most likely already knows about herself.

I return my focus specifically to Emma. "I'm getting a really strong presence of your dog. He or she is deeply devoted to you and is quite an extraordinary creature. Certainly, a worthy companion to you."

I pause briefly. For me, reading cards is part intuition and part groping around with my hands extended, wanting to feel and touch that which is so elusive. "This year will be life-changing. I recommend that you invest in good luggage."

With both feet now on the ground, I'm now a weaver. I pull each card, each thread: gold, yellow, blue, and crimson. "The ten of spades tells me there will be travel in the year ahead. The trip will be a journey over water to a foreign land. You will meet someone. It's slightly unclear to me, but you will travel to meet him. There is a significant amount of strangeness about the situation."

I pause to look at Roxanne and Savannah, then return my gaze to Emma. "There is also a separation from your own belief systems. This may not be easy or comfortable for you. The spiritual realm cautions you not to be judgmental. The time has come for you to work toward healing the wounds of those who came before you. You will need the assistance of many to accomplish your goals. You should not isolate yourself this year. It is as though, through you, the world will be a smaller and better place."

I meditate on the image of the joker and choose my next words wisely. "The joker represents a trickster figure. The trickster's role is to bring truth and enlightenment, but he often does so in an unorthodox manner. You may find yourself emotionally taxed and pushed beyond your perceived limits. In moments like these, it is recommended that you keep a sense of humor and know that you are capable of the challenge. We tend to forget that change can bring tremendous growth."

I lift the upside-down king of spades, right the card, and contemplate its meaning. I then pick up the jack of hearts and hold the two cards next to each other. I feel the weight of the message as though it lives in my own bones. I stop and look at Emma. "There's more."

Emma looks at me with a mixture of apprehension and intrigue. Like a moth drawn to light, she can't resist the hypnotic pull.

"I want you to go on," she says.

It has taken me years of divination experience to trust myself, to trust the divine, and to take a running leap of faith. This, *this*, is why I don't read for strangers. Later, when I'm alone, I will contemplate the fate of the stallions and my hand in setting them free. This is a tremendous responsibility, not one that I take lightly. Such is my destiny to navigate the conscious and the unconscious, the

13

seen and unseen world. I'm a zebra who roams the land attempting to reconnoiter paradox—even in my own skin.

"This king of spades, it's hard to get a clear read on him. He is standing in the shadows. I believe he is your father. You would have had a trying relationship with him. Spade people are smart, but they can be narcissistic. The queen of diamonds and the king of spades would see things differently, and they would lock horns in a power struggle. I believe your father has passed."

I look up at Emma. The expression on her face confirms my intuition. Emma glances at Roxanne and Savannah. They clearly know her family background.

"Actually, that probably is my father. He died two years ago. He wasn't very present in my life," replies Emma.

I pull the crimson thread through the tapestry, weaving the story for Emma, creating a dimension, a depth that previously had not existed. "Your dad really loved his red sports car. It made him extremely happy. He wants me to tell you this so you will believe what I'm about to say. It wasn't that he didn't love you. He had always hoped for another son, and the wounds of *that* situation never really healed for him."

Emma is wide-eyed. "I don't have a brother, only a sister."

I am not dissuaded. The image comes to me like a dream which reveals itself through the mists. I close my eyes and wait in humble reverence, allowing the silence to permeate my being. I know I'm at the altar where all that is holy, divine, and sacred *patiently longs* to be honored. It is a moment when the borderlands between time and worlds are revealed. The story is now before me, clear and visible. Truth itself is the elixir.

I look into Emma's eyes. "This information may not have had any other way to reveal itself to you. Your brother lives somewhere overseas. I believe he would be older than you. By virtue of this, it also means there was a woman your father was involved with." The energy in the room shifts to an uncomfortable silence.

Roxanne breaks the spell. "Emma, is it possible?"

Emma tries to find her way through this unexpected labyrinth. "My dad *was* stationed in Korea," she says, hesitatingly. "But I have to say, I find this very hard to believe. I don't think such a thing could have been kept a secret all these years."

I look at Emma with compassionate wisdom. "I understand your resistance. I want to honor your feelings and reaction. I believe the truth has been locked away in a box. Your father *chose* to take the key with him when he died. There are cycles of life just as there are cycles of nature. If you choose to pursue this, you must be prepared for times of darkness in your soul."

I feel my own heart open to Emma. I imagine the courage this journey will require. I know how fate has a way of shape-shifting our lives, how the landscape of our hearts can quickly change. Transformation—no longer an option—becomes a necessity.

"Emma, whatever adversity comes your way will also bear the fruits of wisdom. The darkness of winter will be followed by the abundant growth of spring. There is also free will. Life often presents us with unexpected paths. We can choose to take them or not; it is up to you. You will choose to do what is right for you and therefore what is also right for your brother."

Emma leans back on the couch and rubs her brow. She closes her eyes.

"Are you all right?" Roxanne asks in concern.

Emma appears to be accessing old archives in her psyche. "Yeah, I'm all right."

Savannah moves to the edge of the couch. "What about the red car?"

"It was a red Jaguar. He and my mother owned it when they lived in Germany. He had a favorite saying: "I like fast cars, fast dogs, and fast women—not necessarily in that order."

Savannah begins to laugh. "Oooooo weeee…you know what that says about your mamma…"

"She *was fast!*" replies Roxanne with dramatic flair. Everyone laughs. Savannah and Roxanne try to lighten the energy. It is, after all, a birthday party, and they want Emma to be happy.

Emma sits silently, reflecting.

"It may take me some time to think about this." Emma looks into my eyes. "Thank you, Amber."

I think about Roxanne coming to the book signing and inviting me here. I think about how I steer clear of personal invitations from strangers and birthday parties like this one. But in this moment—*without any doubt*—I know this is exactly where I am meant to be. In the depths of my soul, I know that Emma has a brother, and I also know she will find him.

Emma Carter

Driving home, the freeway seems more congested than it should be. I opt for a serene route and choose Stanton Street. I pass my favorite coffee shop, Jenny's, which is all buttoned-up for the night. The patio tables are stacked on top of each other, which gives a rather lonely feeling to the place. Up ahead, on the north side of the road, searchlights beam into the sky as if there is some sort of Hollywood film opening. This type of event is incongruent with this part of town. As I get closer, I realize it is the grand opening of a new restaurant. The parking lot is filled with cars. The restaurant name is all lit up in bright neon lights: In-hwa Kim's Korean House of Blessings.

    I pull over, dumbstruck by the coincidence. What is the chance that I discover a new Korean restaurant on the night of Amber's reading? It is a hub of activity. People come and go out of the front door, and I watch the searchlights and contemplate their meaning. It is clear I'm being beckoned into a new story that is rapidly unfolding. Having spent a great deal of my life analyzing story, I certainly understand the structure of a narrative. One of the most beloved and enduring themes is that of the hero. Some heroes embrace their destiny without any hesitation; others are ambiguous and reluctant. A wisdom comes to reluctant heroes, simply because they can imagine the cost of the endeavor. They do not take it lightly. In this circumstance, *I am a reluctant heroine.* This is a minefield of complicated emotions about my father, who he was, and what my responsibility is to him. I am both attracted and repelled. I intuitively know I will go back and forth—like a teeter-totter—until I find my place of balance with a truth that is genuinely and authentically mine.

I gather myself and head home. The silence in the car is a welcome companion as I reflect on Amber's reading. Deep in my heart, I know that her revelation is entirely possible. My father was already married when he met our mother. After my mother, he would have two more wives. He collected women and children along the way like a gypsy under a wandering star.

I can't say I had a complicated relationship with my father—the truth is—I hardly had *any* relationship with him. What we did have was due to my efforts as an adult. By the time he died, I considered us friends, which was a huge accomplishment on my part. Of course, I'd had years of therapy. Each memory of him was acknowledged, touched, and then folded up and put away like clothes stored in a trunk.

Once, in a rare, self-revealing moment, my father told me about a relationship he had with a Korean woman during the war. He showed me her photos. He didn't need to tell me he loved her and always would. It was clear. His face was an open book, and it was easy for me to read every word and see between every line. I turned each page, hungry to experience something I'd never seen before: pure, unedited truth. He made no attempt to conceal his emotions. He had a favorite picture of her; I took it after he died.

Tonight at my party, I kept that information to myself. There is no need to parade his past for public consumption and judgment, which would result only in expectations placed on me. Besides, if there was a brother, he had never tried to contact our family. If Amber was right, my father had chosen to die with his secret intact. Shouldn't I honor his wishes?

In the time I drive home, I'm irritated. *Honestly, what was Roxanne thinking, hiring a psychic!* I put my key into our front door and balance an armful of gifts. I'm happy to be home, happy to be surrounded by a world I have worked to create, a world that is known to me. *If I wanted to go to a psychic, for God's sake, I wouldn't have waited forty-four years!*

"Honey, where are you?" I call out to my husband, Parker.

"I'm in the kitchen," he replies.

I unload my packages on the living room couch and walk into the kitchen. Parker looks tired. His shirt is pulled out of his pants and unbuttoned at the top. His brown hair has been ruffled as if he just ran his hands over his head to massage away a headache. At nearly fifty-three years old, he still shows traces of boyhood. Like now, a vulnerable child rises to the surface of his face. He was always handsome, and his good looks have not faded with age. If anything, he has become more attractive.

Parker has a Perrier in his hand and a half-eaten sandwich on the counter. A mayonnaise jar and two types of mustard are open along with the rye bread package.

19

A dirty knife lies abandoned next to the deli meat. The kitchen reflects urgent, late-night eating. Argos, our dog, intently watches his master. With anxious eyes, he acknowledges my presence, but the smell of corned beef has seduced him beyond his ability to formally greet me.

Parker sets down his drink and embraces me. I put my arms around him, taking comfort in our predictable world. Perhaps I linger longer than usual.

"Are you all right?" he asks, looking into my eyes. "You don't seem too happy. How was your birthday party?"

I hesitate. *How was my party?* "Well...it was intriguing and somewhat inappropriate."

Parker looks surprised. "How could your birthday party be inappropriate?

Suddenly I feel more tired than I should. "I'm sure Roxanne had good intentions, but she hired a psychic to do card readings."

"Carl Jung was a proponent of divination. So was Marie-Louise von Franz."

"That may be, but I'm not. I don't believe that stuff." I move out of his arms, go to the fridge and grab a Perrier for myself. I turn to look at him as I unscrew the top. "The psychic brought up issues about my father." I take a sip of the mineral water. The carbonation bites my tongue. "I'm just going to forget about it, so it's not worth going into. I think I'll head to bed. Did you work late?"

"I did." He pauses and looks concerned. "I'm sure you'll feel better after a good night's sleep. I guess it was a good thing Roxanne's party wasn't on your actual birthday. We'll try to make up for it tomorrow night."

I smile at my husband.

"Emma, I'm so sorry that I have to go into the office on your birthday," he says to me, looking genuinely disappointed.

"It's okay, really. I don't want you to worry about it."

"Your sister called. She'll be here around nine in the morning. Bob and Suzanne also called. They wanted to say happy birthday and suggested we have dinner." Parker chooses a piece of corned beef and offers it to Argos. His jaws snap closed on the meat, his tongue licks his chops, and urgent, desperate whining ensues.

I'm relieved by the change in subject. "Great. Where are we going?"

"They want you to choose. Suzanne chose the restaurant last time. I think we're going to be looking at a lot of photos from their trip."

I feel my emotional teeter-totter gently lift, my feet attempt to remain on the ground. I am gently suspended, my toes hover just above the earth. I surrender, just a little.

"How ironic. I just passed a new restaurant on the way home. A Korean one. I'll think about it, perhaps that might be an interesting option," I say as we exchange goodnight kisses.

"Sounds good." He returns to his half-eaten sandwich.

In record speed, I get ready for bed, crawl under the covers, and prop pillows behind my head. I take the television remote, turn on the TV, and begin to flip through TiVo. I decide to resume watching *The Wizard of Oz*. A bit of nostalgic fantasy might be just the thing I need. I nestle down into the covers as Dorothy admires her ruby slippers. Dorothy shifts her foot ever so gently to the right and then to the left, the glimmering shoes catch the light. Glinda, the Good Witch of the North, sways in her beautiful pink gown and holds her wand. Glinda's gentle voice and presence are a balm for my soul. I can feel myself drifting into sleep and do not resist. The dream world comes through the open window; it carries the night air infused with blooming jasmine from the garden. The curtain gently lifts with its presence.

I am in my own backyard, barefoot and dressed in my nightgown. I hear a gentle voice and look up. It appears to be Glinda, but it is actually Amber in Glinda's clothes. Amber is equally enchanting.

Amber softly sways in her beautiful gown. "Often life presents us unexpected paths," she says. "You can choose to take them or not; it's up to you. You choose what is right for you, and therefore, what is also right for your brother."

Amber gently lifts her wand, transforming my backyard into a large, magical vista. Flowers bloom everywhere. Suddenly a yellow brick path appears. It splits in two directions: one way branches left, the other right. An old wooden sign with two arrows reads: "This Way—That Way." Next to the path stands the Lion, tail in hand, the Scarecrow, looking childlike, and the Tin Man with an axe, but each one has my face.

They are, in fact, all me.

In-sook Lee
June 24, 1955
Teague, Korea

I waited many moons for Randall to return with my heart. The sun made its way across the sky, and spring turned into summer. Blossoms withered, replaced by gold leaves, and the dormancy of winter took up residency within me.

I can no longer bear to listen for the sound of a propeller or scan the sky and hope that Randall will return. Now I only hear the cries of Sang-ho, my baby. I must find love within myself and within Sang-ho, whose eyes hold a new future and whose past will forever haunt me with thoughts of what might have been. How can one man give so much and take so much?

My sister, Min-sook, says this child will be devoted to me. But a sad foreshadowing falls across her face when she speaks of such things. An unspoken destiny entwines him and me, like the roots of two trees, unseen to the eye, yet beneath the surface nature has made one.

Emma Carter
My Birthday

♦

The morning sunlight pours through the kitchen windows like a songbird intent on being heard. Homegrown roses overflow a crystal vase on the counter: Double Delight, Peace, Tournament of Roses, Abe Lincoln, and Rio Samba are in their glory. A deep wave of contentment flows over me. Next to my teacup is a note from Parker: "Happy Birthday, Darling. I'll be home in the afternoon. I love you." Argos howls at me as I fill the kettle for morning tea. Mixed feelings about my birthday party begin to creep back into my mind. The doorbell rings and interrupts my thoughts.

Sarah Carson

I ring Emma's doorbell. I stand with three birthday balloons tied to my hand and two birthday gifts held in the other, one gift from me and one from our mother. My purse slips off my shoulder as I turn to lock the car with the remote. *Come on, Emma, open the door...*

I found Emma's gift in an antique shop in Summerland. I was passing time before meeting my friend Kathy for lunch. The owner was unpacking a box of treasures purchased from an estate in Montecito. Evidently, the people had been world travelers and avid collectors of china. When she pulled this cup and saucer from a sea of newspaper, I knew it was meant to be Emma's. This is the best gift I've ever given my sister, and I can't wait for her to open it.

While the majority of the world marches to the frantic pace of double cappuccinos, Emma and Parker have stayed deeply rooted in the ancient ritual of tea. Emma owns an impressive collection of cups, and she uses them all, not wanting to select just one. She reminds me of a mother afraid of favoring one child over another.

Emma is my younger sister by four years. We are very different people and live dissimilar lives. I know when her front door opens that I will be greeted by an impeccably clean house: everything in its place, no toys to trip over, no stack of yesterday's news, no smell of animals and no shouting children. *How can they bear to live here?* It is simply too sterile. I love my sister, but she's anal.

I happily talk about anything, while she is the more introverted one. *Never* let her brevity fool you. Although she says only five words, a full symphony of thought plays behind them. I call her The Queen of Understatement, and to this day, she still wears the crown.

As a child, she would spend hours writing in her journal, completely content with her own company. When she finished writing, she would carefully lock up all her words, dreams, and inner secrets. Then she would hide the key. It drove me nuts. I wanted to know everything! Once I found her diary key hidden in her Barbies' wardrobe, but in the end I never used it. I am sure she still keeps a journal somewhere in this house. The ink is fresh, the diary's locked, and the key lies hidden.

Emma opens the door. She looks great for forty-four, no lines and hardly any wrinkles.

I break out in song. *"Happy birthday to you…happy birthday to you…happy birthday dear Emma, happy birthday to you!"* We embrace, and I hand her the balloons and gifts.

Emma is all smiles. "Thank you, Sarah. I'm so glad you're here. I just had the kettle on. How about some tea and breakfast?"

"Just tea. I already ate," I say and step into the house.

Emma and Parker have one of those modern homes with an open floor plan. The spacious kitchen reveals the dining room and most of the living room. Consequently, I can't help but notice that the dining room table is set with beautiful white linens, tall candles, and formal china.

"Boy, you didn't waste any time," I say to her.

Emma pauses and smiles as she looks at the table. "Parker must have set it last night."

Disgusting, truly disgusting. I'm lucky to get pizza delivered. Last year on my birthday we watched *Survivor* and took bets on who would be voted off the island. I keep my editorial comments to myself.

I turn to Emma. "One of these gifts is from Mom. She sent me a box of things for the boys and put your gift in with it."

"Thank you. I'll save it for later," Emma responds.

Emma sets the gifts on the kitchen counter and ties the balloons to a bar stool. She pulls two place settings from the cupboard and retrieves my favorite teacup. I can't help but notice the bouquet of roses. "Let me guess: the bouquet is from Parker?"

"Well, actually it is. The roses are from our garden."

"How did you get so lucky with Parker?" I'm trying to be funny, but part of me is truly curious.

Laughing, Emma responds, "Lifetimes of good karma. It's the only explanation."

She must be right. I internally vow to polish my tarnished karma. Emma finishes making toast and boils the hot water. The house is so quiet that I know Parker isn't home. "Is Parker working on your birthday?"

"He had to meet with dissertation advisees. It couldn't be postponed; it has to do with a grant proposal. He must have left early. I didn't even hear him get up."

Emma rinses out the teapot with hot water and proceeds to make tea. The timing for her present couldn't be better.

"I'd like you to open your gift," I say, as I pass the box to her. "I was hoping to catch you before you had your morning tea."

The antique shop outdid itself. The gift is exquisitely wrapped. The paper is a leopard pattern surrounded by a beautiful black satin bow. This caliber of gift wrapping is beyond me; tissue and a Hallmark bag from Long's Drug Store is my style. Emma knows this, and she looks at me and smiles. "It's beautiful, Sarah."

She slowly unwraps the gift and savors the unveiling. Bow and paper removed, she lifts the lid off the box. Emma carefully parts the tissue to reveal the ornate teacup and saucer. In a slow and sacred way, Emma removes her gift from the box and holds the cup up to admire it. Painted on the porcelain is an Asian woman illuminated by gold. There are two men, one on either side of her—both look to her in reverence. The saucer has the larger image of the three together; the cup bears a smaller rendition. The china is museum quality and had a price tag to match. Emma is speechless. *I knew she would love it!*

I walk over to my sister, take the cup from her hand and hold it up to the light. In the very bottom of the cup, there is a portrait of an Asian woman. The portrait, like a relief sculpture, has been created with varying layers of white porcelain. The craftsmanship is impeccable, the detail remarkable. The woman's hair is pulled back into a tight bun, and she wears a kimono. Her stare is piercing, and her eyes appear to communicate from some other realm.

I turn to look at Emma. "She's the reason I bought the cup. Isn't she amazing?"

"Yes, she is. I've never seen anything like it." Emma's voice sounds anxious. She pauses, as if collecting herself. "Thank you, Sarah."

I hand the cup back to her, and she carefully sets it on the saucer.

"Emma, I want you to drink from your new birthday cup."

"Oh no, I couldn't," she replies, acting as if I'm asking for an insurmountable task.

"I bought it for you to use, not just look at."

"It's so beautiful, it's too good to use. I'll just put it somewhere safe."

There is no use fighting over the gift. I know my sister well enough to recognize that her heels are digging through the tile floor. She picks up the cup, with slightly shaking hands, and exits the kitchen. The cup rattles in the saucer. Emma walks with such methodical steps that you'd think she held a nuclear bomb. She walks to the china cabinet in the dining room and opens the glass door. Ever so carefully, she places the cup in a prominent location, shuts the glass door, and secures the latch.

Emma looks at the cup through the glass. "There… now it's safe."

What the hell is up her ass? Wonder Woman has saved the world from atomic disaster. Within the china cabinet, the international threat has been contained. Our children, and their children, will live in peace—safe from the nuclear teacup.

I watch her. "Emma…"

She turns to look at me, "Yes?"
"How was the psychic?"

Emma Carter

I look at Sarah, stunned. "The psychic?"

Sarah glares at me as if my mental stability is in question. "Yeah, you know, the one that Roxanne hired for your birthday." My sister raises her eyebrows and tilts her head, her sarcasm wordlessly displayed.

I walk back to the kitchen. "You knew about her?"

"Yes, we all knew. It was only a surprise to you. Roxanne thought you wouldn't want to do it if she gave you the option."

I pause while trying to come to terms with being the focal point of a conspiracy. "Roxanne was right. I would have said no." I feel a bad mood begin to rise.

"Emma, it was supposed to be fun and different."

"Oh…it was different all right."

Sarah rests her head in her hand. Her face pleads. "Come on. Tell me. I'm dying to know what happened. Of all days for Iain to come down with the flu, I was really disappointed I had to cancel."

I know that surrender is inevitable, so I start at a safe place. "The psychic told Savannah that her romance with Brian looks promising for marriage, and Roxanne got advice on a pending job promotion."

"What about you?" she asks, as I pour her a cup of tea.

"She said that Argos is devoted to me and a really great companion."

Sarah begins to laugh out loud. "Well, that is a revelation! I wonder what she would say about our gerbils."

I can't help but to laugh myself, as it does sound rather ridiculous. Slowly, I inch toward the truth. "She said that travel is in my future and that I should invest in luggage. She told me that I appreciate beauty, and that my home is a sanctuary."

Sarah is all smiles and bright eyed. "Yeah...I could have told you all that, and I'm not a psychic. I was hoping for a little more...*juice.*"

The truth is, I don't want to tell her, and I don't exactly know why. I pour myself a cup of tea, using the cup Parker set out for me. My words come out reluctantly. "She brought up issues about Dad."

Sarah squiggles up her nose like she is a rabbit. "Dad?"

My voice fills with hope. "Dad isn't juicy enough for you?"

Sarah shakes her head. "No, not really. It isn't what I had in mind." She looks disappointed.

I'm relieved. I smile at my sister and feel as though an asteroid has just moved through my atmosphere, and with the grace of God, I stepped aside and dodged it. I allow the silence to linger and take a sip of tea.

Sarah seems satisfied. "I guess I didn't miss much after all." Her eyes meet mine. "How are you spending your day?"

"I'm going to have lunch with Loraine and help her with the birds."

Sarah is not surprised. I spend a considerable amount of time with Loraine.

"We have a hawk almost ready for release and possibly an owl."

Although my sister is interested in my work with injured birds, I know it seems decadent to her. To Sarah, I symbolize the "double income, no kids" stereotype. She thinks my hours of volunteer work are self-indulgent. Her time and energy must go in other directions.

She looks at her watch. "I need to pick up Max. He's got practice in an hour." She stops and looks at me. "Before I forget, Mom told me you're giving this year's graduation speech. We'd like to go."

I feel embarrassed that she learned this from our mother and not directly from me. "I haven't had a chance to tell you, Sarah, but I hope you can attend. Parker will be in Boston, at a conference. Graduation is the first Saturday in June. I'll give you the details as it gets closer."

"All right, we'll plan on it." Sarah gets up from her chair and takes a last sip of tea. "I hope you have a great birthday, Emma."

"Thank you, and thank you for the beautiful teacup. It's amazing."

"I'm glad you like it."

"I love it, Sarah."

We walk to the front door together and exchange a good-bye hug. I stand in the doorway and watch Sarah walk to her car. We give each other a final wave good-bye, and I shut the door. Alone again, I go to the living room and turn on the stereo. I sort through our music collection and find a Ray Charles CD. I turn on the stereo, pop in the disc, and skip ahead to the song *Somewhere Over the Rainbow*. I walk back to the kitchen and sing the words, inspired by his soulful rendition of an old classic.

Standing at the kitchen window, I admire the backyard, which is a blooming bouquet of color. I have a sudden sense of déjà vu but can't capture the elusive memory. Was it a dream? I feel as though I repeatedly drop a bucket into a deep, dark well and pull up nothing, yet I know that water once existed there. Dreams can be mercurial—wanting to be experienced on their terms. The memory is gone, dried up within the bowels of the earth. On this day, I will never taste the water I long for from the well.

Loraine North

In one grand sweep, God took my husband and two sons. A trucker, driving south on 101, fell asleep at the wheel and crossed the freeway just below Gaviota. My grief was unrelenting. It was all I could do to get out of bed, raise my head, or sit straight in a chair. Suicide was a reasonable option, except for one thing: I'd taken in wounded wild birds for rehabilitation, and I now had sole responsibility for their care. Their needs gave me a focus and purpose. The sharp-shinned hawk was ready for release, the osprey would need to be returned to Lake Cachuma in the Santa Ynez Valley, and the Merlin falcon required medicated salve for his gaping wound.

How did I begin to live again? For me, it happened by healing wounded birds one at a time. Each bird released back into its natural habitat helped mend my own torn and tattered heart. By making contributions to heal nature, the earth and its creatures, I prayed that God would heal me, too. Thirty years later, I'm still devoted to the birds.

As fate would have it, my work as a veterinarian assistant at the Francene Veterinarian Clinic prepared me for this calling. It also gave me access to medical supplies and a compassionate veterinarian. That first year, my backyard sprouted aviaries like mushrooms in springtime.

With each bird I accepted, I worked toward trusting nature and its cycles of life. Even with my best efforts, many birds died. I've lost numerous red-shouldered hawks. They don't do well in captivity. They are high-strung, and the confinement of the cage breaks their spirit and eventually their body. There have been countless others: hit by cars, poisoned by chemicals, injured by falling trees. I've tried to accept that loss is part of life—certainly, it is part of this work.

Within two years, I started a nonprofit called The Raptor Rehabilitation Center. Today I have twenty-eight owls, hawks, and falcons, ten of which are baby barn owls. This undertaking is made possible with the help of volunteers and donations from individuals and ecologically minded companies. Some birds will be here for the rest of their lives, like the Cooper's hawk with one wing, the American kestrel with only one foot, or the great horned owl who is unable to fly due to a neurological problem.

Spring is my busiest time of year. The wind and rain dislodge nests from trees. Year after year it's the same story: orphaned barn owls.

Nearly every species can boast about the beauty of its infants: wide-eyed, innocent, soft and cuddly, and charmingly unstable on their feet. Baby barn owls, however, will never win any awards or be photographed for glossy pages of a birding calendar. To see a newly hatched barn owl, one takes a step back and says under his or her breath, "Good god!" and then feels guilty for such judgmental thoughts. Their heads wobble on necks too delicate to hold the weight, their dark eyes bulge, and

38

sparse feathers barely cover their grey flesh. Their tiny wings move up and down as if attached to a mechanical apparatus. In addition, they display early signs of a demanding temperament.

Feeding the baby barn owls requires the help of every volunteer and friend I have. Each owlet must be wrapped in a towel to protect its wings. Food is placed at the back of its throat with long tweezers, while its beak rhythmically opens and closes as it gratefully accepts food from a surrogate parent. It is in this very act of the feeding, with the owls wrapped in swaddling, that the love occurs. There is some osmosis—an exchange between species—that transforms these awkward little creatures into reciprocates of devotion.

In regard to my home, I've lived here since the late 1950s. It lies at the end of a busy street in Santa Barbara. The house was old and dilapidated when we purchased it. It was renovated over the years and provided the framework for our stories: the birth of our first son, his learning to ride a bicycle, and Rover, our family dog. My husband's professional accomplishments and my joy of being a mother. Then our second son arrived, his love of swimming and surfing, the stray cat that found its way into our hearts, and my work at the veterinary clinic. Over the years, it was the land we came to appreciate—our little corner in the midst of the city's pace. The house sits on an acre and borders an unbuildable, sloping hillside. At today's prices, I could never afford such property. Since the deaths of my husband and sons, my focus of renovation and construction has been solely for wounded birds. As the years pass, I care less and less about the inside of the house. My life's work is now focused outside—outside the house and perhaps outside of me as well.

I stand looking at my backyard, anticipating lunch with Emma. The day is beautiful. The sky is clear blue with a few random clouds. A patio table, with its large sheltering umbrella, sits in the middle of the yard. Unlike the typical backyard, mine is filled with the calls of various birds. It is never quiet, and I am never alone. Today the table is formally set. Emma is joining me for her birthday lunch. Despite the fact that I offered to cook, she insisted on stopping by our local deli to get lunch.

Emma is about the age my sons would be if they had lived. I often find myself wondering about them in relationship to her. They would have liked her, maybe even loved her. She could have been my daughter-in-law. She could have been at my table for Thanksgiving, Christmas and Easter. Instead, I'm at her table for the holidays. Sometimes family isn't connected by blood or marriage. Sometimes love moves beyond boundaries, and family comes in unexpected ways. I love Emma as though she were my own daughter. For this, I'm eternally grateful. You see, the wild birds, they not only healed my heart, but they also gave me the daughter I'd always dreamed of.

Parker Carter

♦

Academics run in my family. My love of learning came through my father. He's a philosophy professor at the University of Minnesota. My father's brother, my uncle, is also an academic. He conducts medical research for the University of Portland. Both of them are old enough to retire, but each refuses to surrender to a life of gardening and volunteer work.

Throughout my childhood, my father's face was happily buried in books as he worked on new insights of Plato. Every night at the dinner table, he perfected his classroom lectures. Between mouthfuls of mashed potatoes and gravy, my father would elaborate on Aristotle and Socrates. His lectures were peppered with memorized poetry of Homer. He playfully demanded our full attention and wouldn't tolerate any "straying minds." As my father took a breath between inspirations, my mother would turn to me, smile and wink. She made no attempts to conceal our silent exchange. My father found this very amusing. Year after year my mother and I sat fascinated by my father's abduction into a world we watched only through a glass window.

Despite his many eccentricities, my mother adored him and basked in the warmth of his perpetual sunshine.

At night I would lie in bed and listen to their muffled words and laughter. My father loved to chase my mother around their bedroom. In my mind, I could see her touching the top of the chair as she tried to dodge him; then came my father's inevitable conquest and my mother's surrender with peals of laughter. Although I never understood what was going on, I knew they were happy. I never doubted their love for each other or their devotion to me.

Every Friday evening faculty from the department came to the house. They sat drinking liquid amber from crystal glasses and blowing smoke rings into the air. They were a jolly group, delighted to be in each other's company, thrilled to have a passionate audience for their evolving theories. As a small boy, I would sneak down the stairs wearing pajamas, sit unseen in the hallway wanting only to hear their voices and my father's place amid the chatter. As I grew older, I was allowed to sit quietly in the room. I attentively watched the movements and gestures of those who had become renowned in their field.

When the '60s came, my mother broke out of her pencil skirts like a T. rex coming out of its shell. My father, aghast, gradually got used to the idea that her houndstooth suit was gone and wearing a bra was optional. My mother took to the streets wanting equal rights for women. She became an advocate and fund-raiser for the first Planned Parenthood in Minneapolis. She believed a woman's right to abortion was as essential as air itself and fundamental in reclaiming feminine power. My life was profoundly shaped by both my parents, a love of classical philosophy through my father and a deep respect for women and a feminist perspective through my mother.

42

Later, I worked toward my own PhD in philosophy from NYU. On trips home, I found my place among the Friday evening philosophers. I no longer sat quietly in their presence. I blew my own smoke rings prior to sitting in their circle. It was the late 1970s. I was a young man, confident in myself and eager to forge my way in academia. My father's pride in me was evident, as was his interest when I spoke of Kant's *Dreams of a Spirit Seer.* He sat quietly in his worn leather chair, now listening to my voice and trying to assess its place within the circle.

I earned my second PhD in psychology from UC Berkeley in the 1980's. That's where I met Emma. I was on my way to meet my dissertation advisor. I'd just purchased a cup of coffee and was drinking it as I walked. Emma came around a corner, busy talking with someone, ran right into me, and spilled coffee all over my clothes. I couldn't say it was love at first sight.

We met again two months later at a party of a mutual friend. Emma's cheeks turned bright red as we were formally introduced. I found this charming. It didn't hurt that she was also gorgeous. Her thick brown hair fell to the center of her back. Although she had a body that she could have advertised, she didn't. Emma's shyness was captivating. With every word I spoke, I felt as though I was dangling a piece of yarn in front of a cat, enticing her to engage with me. She had moved to California from Wisconsin and was pursuing her master's degree in English.

Truth be told, I wanted to have sex with her. As the party grew, the kitchen became crowded and space was a premium. My body found its way next to Emma's. I rested

43

my arm above her on the top of the refrigerator; I leaned in and told her I would always be grateful for the coffee stain. The coffee, all over my clothes, endeared me to my advisor in a way that hadn't previously existed. Our work together had significantly changed since that meeting. In the weeks that followed the mishap, I had come to define that day as auspicious.

Emma laughed at this, unsure if she should actually believe me. She tilted her head. Her brown eyes sparkled at me, her skin was flawless, and her lips full and promising. In that moment I knew I had her, and it was only a matter of time before my fingers ran through her hair and across her bare skin. What I didn't expect is that I would fall in love with her.

I left the party that night without her number. I didn't even ask for it. We had mutual friends, and I knew contacting her would be easy. I went home and worked on my dissertation until four in the morning. I channeled my sexual energy into writing. That time in my life became synonymous with Emma. I pursued her between each page of my dissertation. Gradually, she surrendered to me. After hours of kissing on the couch, I went home to write on Sigmund Freud. As I progressed with my research, I rewarded myself with her further seduction. Emma respected my self-imposed restraint and became my biggest advocate. With each chapter completed, another piece of clothing came off. C. G. Jung had never made so much sense. Before long we were down to our underwear. I was an ambitious student, studying every nuance of her body, the way she smelled, her hair cascading across her shoulders. I intimately knew every inch of her.

We had done everything sexually *but* have intercourse. At first, the slow pace appealed to Emma, but near the end she too was tortured by it. As my dissertation conclusion drew near, the sexual anticipation was overwhelming. I resorted to phoning Emma in the last three weeks of my writing. During that time, we perfected the art of phone sex. Anything previously unsaid had now been elaborated with great detail. I had never wanted a woman more. My experience with Emma was unlike anything I had ever known in my previous dating history. When I finished the last chapter, Emma met me at her door breathless, buttons went flying, and we nearly broke the bed frame. In nine months of foreplay, I had finished my second PhD and now had a steady girlfriend with a big smile on her face.

That Christmas I took Emma home to Minneapolis to meet my parents. My mother had replaced the twin bed in my room with a larger one so that Emma and I could sleep together. The new bed was fitted with beautiful linens and a fluffy down comforter. If anyone knew the value of a great sex life, it was my mother, and she always wanted the best for her son.

Emma and I slept in my room surrounded by my football trophies, various sports ribbons, and memorabilia from the '60s and early '70s. My room felt like the Smithsonian of my life. Every time I went home, I felt as though I should be paying an admission fee in the doorway and wear a small round pin for the duration of my stay. Although the rest of the house had changed in minor ways, my room was always the same, frozen in time. I encouraged my parents to make my room into a den, library, or a second guest room. They were content to leave it exactly the way it looked years ago. It didn't take a PhD in psychology to understand the symbolic meaning of their actions. As a grown man it was an odd experience. My old Panasonic clock radio still worked like a charm. When I graduated from high school, my parents bought a great stereo system for me to take to college. My original phonograph player sat in the corner, recently dusted. A few lingering vinyl records were stacked next to it: Buffalo Springfield, The Byrds, Traffic, and Creedence Clearwater Revival. My big speakers anchored each corner of the room.

That first night, while the snow fell outside the window, Emma and I made love listening to "Midnight Rider" by The Allman Brothers, the bass guitar gently vibrating the room, just like the old days. Outside, the house was decorated with Christmas lights that blinked on and off, casting a holiday glow into the room. I felt like I was seventeen again and having sex with my fantasy girl. Reliving my adolescence had never felt so fulfilling. The only thing missing was my bong, which I had kept hidden in the closet for my trips home. I guess even my parents had their limitations.

Over the years I had brought women back to Minneapolis to meet my parents, but Emma was different, and they intuitively knew this. My parents loved her. What wasn't to love? Emma was respectful, smart, and beautiful. But most important, Emma and I adored each other. Although my parents kept their opinion to themselves, I knew they began to hear the pitter-patter of little feet across the kitchen floor.

46

Christmas was a huge success. It was during that holiday that I came to understand my life had taken a new course. Emma was now an integral part of contributing to my happiness. I couldn't imagine my life without her. I had breathed her into my soul. Without Emma, my life would be diminished. I was smart enough to know this. I had devoted my life to pursuing a higher education. Somehow a woman who had spilt coffee all over me had effortlessly lassoed my heart with astounding precision. *No one was more amazed than me.*

When we returned to Berkeley, I applied for academic teaching positions. Ann Arbor, Michigan, had an opening in the Philosophy Department that sounded promising. I interviewed and then accepted a full-time teaching position to start that fall. Emma finished her degree that spring. We each packed up our separate apartments and filled a U-Haul. We drove out of California and into the Midwest, happy to be starting an adventure together.

A few years later, a former colleague of mine recruited me for the Department of Psychology at the University of California Santa Barbara. I began giving guest lectures there in the early '90s and was hired as core faculty in 2000. Emma and I had been freezing in Ann Arbor and were thrilled to return to the warm California climate.

Like most major universities, UCSB is a large, sprawling place. However, this campus is one of the most beautiful in the nation, perched on a bluff overlooking the Pacific Ocean. Windows run the length of my office, affording me an impressive ocean view; the Channel Islands are clearly visible to the south. It is easy to feel inspired by such a panorama.

The serenity of the view is a welcome reprieve from my office, which reflects varying degrees of chaos. One wall is lined with books: *The Collected Works of C. G. Jung* alongside works by Robert A. Johnson and Marie-Louise von Franz, Marion Woodman, James Hillman, Paul Mahaffey, Darwin L. Miller, Kristie Downing, David Slattery, Genny Paris, and Gaston Bachelard, among others.

I teach one undergraduate class per year and three graduate classes, and I manage research grants. I take a feminist approach to psychology with an ample dose of philosophy. This niche has afforded me a unique position in academia.

I enjoy the students at UCSB, although I do notice that class attendance shrinks when the surf is up. In spring, the scent of suntan lotion permeates the classroom to the point of nausea. Due to the focus of my courses, the majority of my students are female. I keep a professional distance from them to avoid messy allegations of sexual harassment. I've seen more than one career brought down by a college coed lathered in coconut oil. I have no intention of joining the ranks of my once naive colleagues.

The timing of grants often leaves a lot to be desired. Today is Emma's birthday. I wish I could have spent the day with her, maybe gone to the Santa Barbara Museum of Art followed by a leisurely lunch. Instead, I've been here since eight this morning with four grad students, evaluating their research methods. It is now one in the afternoon, and I'm famished. I am fatigued from the work and worn down from hunger. After I take a quick break, I still have three more hours of work ahead of me.

I'm preparing to leave for lunch when my office door abruptly opens and Lauren, a newly minted PhD, walks in. Lauren has the mind of a great scholar; I anticipate that her future work will be recognized internationally. She is also exceptionally beautiful. She is known throughout the department and has been the focus of more than one private conversation.

Lauren hands me a sandwich wrapped in white butcher paper. I'm surprised. "How did you know?"

Lauren smiles. "I just saw Julie. She said you were starving."

"I am starving. Thank you for the sandwich."

Unable to restrain myself, I rip open the paper and take a bite. I reach for my wallet. "Here, let me pay you." I remove a $10 bill and hand it to Lauren.

She looks at the bill, then looks at me and smiles. "You don't need to pay me." She hesitates. "I've been meaning to thank you for helping me get that job in Montana."

"You earned that yourself, Lauren."

"We both know it was your influence that got me the job."

"Your teaching and research skills stand on their own merit," I say to her.

An electric tension fills the room.

Lauren looks at me. "Now that I'm officially graduated, I want to tell you how much I've appreciated you."

I watch her analytically. I hope this won't go where it seems to be heading. I try to normalize the situation. "Lauren, I was a grad student once, too. Let me pay you for the sandwich."

49

My subtle hint to change the subject fails to register. She steps closer to me and stares into my eyes, full of confidence. "There has been something between us for a long time. I know you feel it, too."

Frankly, I do feel it, but what man wouldn't? I've worked with Lauren for five years and have always known that somewhere beneath her calm and collected exterior is a modern-day siren. Today, of all days, I am not prepared for this type of confrontation. I'm exhausted from long hours and a weekend that's not yet over.

Her voice takes on a tone of justification. "By this time next week, I'll be gone."

Lauren steps directly in front of me. She is so close I can smell her. She lifts her chin and slightly arches her back. It is an evocative pose—a beckoning one. She raises one eyebrow and challenges me. "I think it's time we put an end to the sexual tension between us, don't you?"

I wonder how many men have been shipwrecked by her. She strokes my face with her hand, and I hear her siren's song as I plunge to my death.

Argos, the Dog

In this lifetime, I have lived with Emma and Parker since I was nine weeks old. I was a present for Emma and Parker's fifth wedding anniversary. That was ten years ago. Parker wrapped a beautiful red bow around my neck, and I joyfully pranced into Emma's arms, as I have done a thousand times before. I was thrilled to see her. She nestled her face into my fur to breathe me into her soul. I licked her hands and her face, eager to taste her once again. That first moment of being reunited with a loved one is exhilarating, and knowing—*knowing*—we have a whole lifetime together is sheer perfection.

Personally, I enjoy the conveniences of *this* time in history. In many ways it is quite decadent. I have never needed to hunt for my own food or for the food of Emma and Parker. While they are at work, I get on their bed and nestle into the down comforter for my afternoon nap. I treasure being the only pet and the focus of many conversations, random gifts—ridiculous and otherwise—and a significant amount of attention.

It had been a long time since I had seen Emma. My last incarnation had been with Parker in the 1850s. He and I lived in Scotland, on the Isle of Skye. Side by side, we endlessly roamed the Cuillin hills. He was a writer even then. A mystic some said. Our lives were lived in silent contemplation. For a dog, it was a very good life, and I have fond memories of it. For a man, years of silent contemplation is the borderland of loneliness and depression. Yes, it's true; he was revered for his deep wisdom, but that life lived in silence was a penance of destiny. A bit tortured, I must say. To live so alone is not natural. Unknown to him, he was trying to come to terms with leaving Emma behind, vulnerable and pregnant, the lifetime before. It was selfish of him, and on some level he knew this, but I'm getting ahead of myself with this story.

My first life with Emma was lived in what we now know as France. We lived in a small village along the Route des Vin River, not far from Strasburg. Emma's father was a clockmaker. He worked for years in the Notre-Dame Cathedral making an enormous astronomical clock. He spent countless hours in the cathedral, often sleeping on the cold stone floor. When he did come home, his nights were spent gazing at the stars, as if captured under a mysterious spell. He died early, at the age of thirty-two. The year was 1564, his beloved clock not yet finished. After his death, the family moved to Ribeauvillé to live with Emma's grandparents. Emma's grandfather was a gifted gardener, particularly with roses. Although they were poor, they somehow managed to be surrounded by nature's beauty.

It was in the village of Ribeauvillé that Emma and Parker met for the first time. They fell hopelessly in love. Parker's family were wealthy, prominent landowners and winemakers. Emma's family struggled to till the soil. Circumstances made them an unlikely pair. Even as a dog I knew this.

52

It was a time of social upheaval between the Huguenots and the Catholics. In the summer of 1570, Parker was killed fighting for religious beliefs. His body arrived home in the back of a horse-drawn cart. He wasn't alone. Within the pile laid friends and neighbors, their bodies pressed together in lifeless weight. Throughout the village, the wailing of grief was heard for weeks. Emma was left paralyzed by grief. She was also pregnant.

Unwed, she hid the pregnancy. Unwed mothers represented temptation and sin and were considered to be weak in character. They were often stoned to death in the town's center. Only her grandmother knew about the pregnancy. The house was filled with silent observation and whispers in the dark. Paleness spread over Emma's face, as if a ghost had taken up residency. When the baby was ready to be born, Emma, her grandmother, and I, went to the shallows of the river. Emma sank down into the cool, flowing water to give birth. No first breath was ever taken, no cry was heard. We silently stood as we watched the river take the baby, its tiny white body gently twisting and turning with the current of the water. Emma waded out into the river to get a final glimpse of her child. Once gone, she sank down into the bloody mud, her body heaving in anguish. Her grandmother stood on the shore, staring into the distance, her clothes soaked with remorse.

Knowing that his death was a possibility, Parker had entrusted Emma with his beloved falcon. The bird became symbolic to Emma. She felt it was a messenger to the heavens and therefore to Parker and their baby. It was Parker who taught Emma to love birds. And it was Emma who taught Parker that love has its own pair of wings— wings that can easily fly—from one lifetime to another.

Emma Carter

I pull my Jeep into Loraine's driveway and get out of the car. With one hand I take my purse; with the other I grab the brown bag containing lunch from Cantend's Market. Cantend's has the best chicken salad in the world. With fresh ciabatta rolls and cold, marinated asparagus, it creates an award-winning lunch—takeout style.

Loraine's house needs attention. The hedges grow wild, and the grass needs cutting. Empty birdcages line the driveway, sharing the space with random weeds. It is clear that Loraine's time and attention go elsewhere.

Her Craftsman-style home has a large porch on the front of the house. Lucy, Loraine's old yellow lab, sleeps on her outdoor bed. Lucy doesn't hear me as I approach. If I weren't accustomed to her behavior, I would think she had died peacefully in her sleep. I knock on Loraine's front door and then open it. "Loraine, it's me, Emma!" I call into the silent house.

Lucy lifts her head and looks at me, gives a heavy sigh, and then rearranges herself on the bed. I walk into the living room, closing the door behind me.

I've been doing volunteer work with Loraine for the last five years. We met at the Museum of Natural History. She was holding a northern screech owl while talking about her work with wounded birds. One thing led to the next, and before I knew it, I had on kidskin gloves and was holding the tiny owl. The spell was cast—both with Loraine and with wild birds. That particular screech owl remains one of my favorites. He is a full-time resident and won't be returned to the wild due to a broken wing that mended poorly.

"I'm in here," Loraine calls from the kitchen.

I walk through Loraine's living room, which reflects her work. Volunteer information sheets lie on the coffee table alongside reference books. Statues, paintings, and ornaments of birds fill the room. A large birdcage sits in the middle of the floor, covered with a sheet. I hear movement coming from inside the cage. Clearly, a new resident has arrived.

I set down my purse and our lunch in the kitchen. Loraine wears jeans and an untucked blue denim shirt. Her grey hair is wild, like her hedges. She is old enough to be my mother. Despite her casualness, there is an undeniable aura of wisdom that surrounds her. Her beauty lies far below the surface of her skin. Loraine resided in the underworld when her family was killed. Now, emerged from that, she lives her life in a deep state of consciousness.

Loraine has been squeezing lemons by hand. Their husks lie abandoned on the counter. A glass pitcher with lemon slices, sprigs of mint, and ice sits to one side. She rinses off her hands, quickly dries them, and then holds out her arms to me. "Happy birthday, Emma!" she says, wrapping her arms around me. We stand embracing each other. Her body is warm and comforting.

56

"Thank you, Loraine."

"Such devotion, helping me with the birds on your birthday," she says as we release our hold.

"I wouldn't have it any other way! Besides, I brought my favorite lunch." I gesture toward the living room, "What's in the cage?"

"A burrowing owl. I just picked him up—take a look." Loraine's attention returns to the lemonade.

I walk back to the living room, quietly approach the cage, gently lift the sheet, and peer in. The owl perches on a branch. His round yellow eyes stare back at me. He is stunning, with exquisite, fawn-colored, polka-dotted feathers. Breathing heavily, with an open beak, it is clear the bird is traumatized. I put the cover down and return to the kitchen.

"He's beautiful. Where did he come from?" I ask Loraine.

Loraine adds lemon juice and water to the glass pitcher. She glances up at me as she methodically stirs sugar water into the lemonade. "Tiro Canyon Road. He was on the ground jumping around somebody's pool. The house sitter saw him. She managed to cover him with a box so that the neighborhood cats wouldn't kill him." As she stirs the lemonade, slices of lemon and sprigs of mint move round in circles, and the ice clinks against the glass.

"What's wrong with him?"

"I'm not sure. His eyes are tracking well, so that's a good sign. He is unable to fly, though, and does seem to favor one side. I haven't had a chance to look at him closely. I thought I would let him rest quietly, till after lunch." Loraine tastes the lemonade, testing its sweetness.

57

Her eyes twinkle as she smiles at me, insinuating a perfectly balanced flavor.

Loraine nods with her head toward the back door. "Let's sit outside. It's a beautiful day."

Loraine takes the pitcher of lemonade, and I grab the Cantend bag.

I often contemplate my relationship with Loraine. She is the mother I always dreamed of having. She reminds me of the Greek goddess Hestia, who symbolized the home—the hearth. Hestia was a protector of the family and sought social stability. In her own way, Loraine's Hestian qualities manifest by tending the earth and its wild birds. In addition, she nurtures the volunteers who arrive with their own broken wings.

When I am with Loraine working with the birds, I feel content on a very profound level. Naturally, I would love to work with the birds in any setting, but it's Loraine, her wisdom and intuition, that captivates me. Until I met her I hadn't realized that I—myself—needed mothering or that my own wings were in question.

Although my mother is still alive, we have a relationship like that of the cactus wren and the giant saguaro. Somehow, I have managed against all odds, to build a nest in a forbidden place. Her heart is full of thorns—old wounds unresolved, unhealed, and denied. I gingerly navigate around them.

Loraine and I are like two orphans: she lost her children, and I need a mother. There is a balanced simpatico between us.

Outside, the patio table, with a large sheltering umbrella, sits in the middle of the yard. It is beautifully set with floral placemats, crystal goblets for the lemonade, Loraine's good china, and a birthday gift for me. I hardly recognize the table. I am so accustomed to seeing it covered with bird paraphernalia and surrounded by volunteers.

"Loraine, the table is beautiful," I say to her, appreciating her thoughtfulness.

Loraine is delighted that I am so happy. We both sit down. She pours the lemonade.

"You didn't need to get me a gift." I look at her.

"Of course I did. Go on, open it. I can't wait any longer!"

The gift is wrapped in paper patterned with bird feathers. Loraine smiles at me, pleased with herself. I remove the gold ribbon and unwrap the gift. Inside the tissue lies a pair of raptor gloves that extend to the elbow. They are made of heavy tan suede and lined with thick wool. My initials have been ornately embroidered in brown thread on the back of them. They are the most beautiful raptor gloves I've ever seen, clearly custom made. I feel myself choke with emotion.

Loraine reaches over to touch my arm. "This gift is long overdue." With her other hand she gestures to the aviaries. "I couldn't do all this without your help."

Tears form in my eyes and create a pool of saltwater.

She watches me as I slip my hands inside the gloves. I extend my stiff gingerbread arms in front of me. I turn to Loraine, whose own eyes have filled with tears.

My words come out in a whisper, "Thank you, Loraine."

Tears roll down her cheeks. I reach over and wipe them away with my clumsy cookie-cutter hand. I then wipe my own cheeks. Together, our tears blend, the moisture quickly absorbing into the suede.

Love and appreciation are the first stains on the virgin leather. I know that once dry, the glove will forever hold the memory of our lunch under the umbrella, our tears subtly outlined in a ring of saltwater.

Parker Carter

I hear a loud thud hit the window and turn to see the body of a seagull sliding down the glass. A streak of blood mars the pane. Did the bird hear the siren's song and die a death for me?

I grasp Lauren's hand to stop her caress. Rejection shows all over her face, and fury instantaneously follows. With her free hand she slaps me across the face—*hard*.

As I reel from the shock of the blow, there is a knock on my door. Ed, a colleague, steps into my office, oblivious to what's unfolding. He quickly assesses the situation, however, and looks embarrassed.

"Oh, sorry." Ed squints in awkwardness, "Looks like bad timing." He starts to back out of the room.

I look at him. "It's not bad timing." Ed gets the hint and stops in the doorway, shifting his weight back and forth, hands shoved into his pockets.

Lauren's face flushes with anger. She assertively plucks the $10 bill from my hand. Without acknowledging Ed, she stalks out of my office.

Like a ship parting the sea, the anger left in Lauren's wake is palpable. Ed turns to me. "What the hell was that?"

"A rejected woman," I respond flatly.

Ed begins to laugh loudly, "*You rejected Lauren?!* You're more of a man than me. Come on, didn't you think about it, even for two seconds?"

I have an interesting relationship with Ed. We've worked together for many years, and despite the fact that he's a narcissistic womanizer, I've managed to recognize the good in him and consider him a friend. Feeling a bit shell-shocked, I rub my burning face. "I'd rather not say."

Ed is completely entertained. "Well, you let me know when you step off the path so I can make my move on your wife."

I respond with a half-smile. "You're a fucking dog, Ed."

"Yeah, I am. Dr. Dog, that's me. Lauren may be beautiful, but Emma is priceless." He rubs his brow as if to solve a long-held mystery. "Emma is too good for you, and we both know it."

I don't give him the pleasure of a response.

Ed walks over to me and takes a look at my face. "I hate to tell you this, buddy, but I think she drew blood."

I rub my cheek, look at my hand and feel a profound sense of regret. "She must be wearing a ring. This is really bad timing. Today is Emma's birthday."

Ed smiles like the Cheshire Cat. "You poor fool. These are the perils of being so well published. You brought this on yourself."

"You saved me. I owe you one," I say to him.

"Actually, I came to see if you want to get some lunch, but I see you already have a sandwich."

I grab the sandwich and toss it into the trash can. "Let's go." As we leave the office, Ed gives me consolatory slap on the back. After lunch, I will go home. My priorities have taken a sudden turn.

62

Emma Carter

Every culture has beliefs about owls. The Navajo believe they represent ancestral spirits. To the Welsh, they are affiliated with fertility. In ancient Greece, an owl accompanied Athena, the Greek goddess of knowledge, to symbolize her higher wisdom.

Owls have long been associated with sorcery and witchcraft due to their ability to fly silently and see at night. Historically and culturally, owls engender polar opposite reactions: they are deemed sacred and honored—they are feared and hated.

When I began my volunteer work with Loraine, I expected to become enamored of hawks and falcons, which I certainly am, but I never expected to be so captivated by owls. There are more than two hundred different varieties of owls. They range in size from the smallest, the elf owl, about the size of a large sparrow, to the Eurasian eagle owl with its wingspan of up to six feet.

Wearing my new birding gloves, I unlatch the door to an adult barn owl's cage. I brace myself for the intensity of these birds; they are profoundly intimidating. Resting my right hand at the open door of the barn owl's cage, my body blocks his exit. The large owl begins a slow, rhythmic dance, shifting his weight back and forth.

His head turns left and right, a motion that is primitive and hypnotic. Although there is something about this movement that seems seductive—cobra-like—the bird actually is attempting to hear me.

I move my right hand toward him. His powerful talons strike at my glove as he backs into the corner of the cage—daring me in. The barn owl begins his screaming screech. His voice is loud enough to fill a forest, and in this small space the sound is deafening. Time after time he strikes my hand with his talons. My heart pounds in my chest and adrenaline races through my veins. The wrath of nature is undeniable. Make no mistake, inside this small cage a war rages. Although the owl is a fraction of my size and weight, he is a worthy match. Seizing the perfect opportunity, in one quick movement I grab his leg, careful not to injure him. With my other hand, I hold his torso between the legs and support his body. He fights me with every cell in his body, screaming incessantly.

I slowly remove the owl from the cage, taking my time to avoid injuring his wings. Once out, he spreads his wings wide, in full rebellion. With a swift maneuver, the owl strikes at my face with his left wing. I swerve and avoid the intended clip.

Loraine stands next to me, watching.

I quickly glance at her. "I swear, these barn owls come out of the shell angry."

I turn the owl toward Loraine. His titanic wrath now focuses on her. With her gloved hands, she examines the wings and body. She lifts the breast feathers, searching for mites, and checks for evidence of illness.

64

Loraine is completely unfazed by the owl's fury. "He's quite healthy. We'll try him in the large aviary next week. He could be ready for release in a week or two."

Finished with her inspection, Loraine cleans the owl's cage.

The owl, now tired of the struggle, allows his wings to fall to his side. He watches me, suspicious of my intentions. His beak remains open and ready for attack.

In captivity, barn owls have no qualms about expressing their feelings. When I work with barn owls, even the babies, I can't be complacent. They demand full and undivided attention. All large owls can do serious damage to a human if given the opportunity. When I hold a great horned owl, its talons are so strong that its grip actually stops the circulation in my hand. It is easy to imagine how effortlessly this large bird could lift a rabbit off the ground or tear open the flesh of a man.

An owl's intensity intrigues me—its unapologetic expression and exemplary courage in the face of adversity. I believe the animals that we are drawn to have lessons to teach us. At forty-four, I am still striving to attain my night vision and voice. The barn owl is my teacher, and with every interaction I'm altered in some small but meaningful way that moves beyond words.

Loraine lines the cage with fresh paper and steps back. The owl willingly returns to the familiar safety of the container. I quickly shut the door. He looks back at me, resentment still apparent.

Other birders have their life lists (a species list to record sightings) and travel to remote parts of the world to check off the stunning lilac-breasted roller in Africa or the colorful silver-eared mesia in Fraser's Hill, Malaysia. A trek up Cerro de La Muerte in Costa Rica might provide a glimpse of the resplendent quetzal.

You don't need a passport to experience the wonders of birding. We have our prizes here in America as well. Although I consider myself a birder, my life list consists of birds caged due to injury, who still, as Maya Angelou said, "sing." I know one day my focus will change. Loraine and I often talk of taking a trip to Madera Canyon in Arizona in hopes of seeing the elegant trogon. Perhaps by then I will have my Zeiss binoculars, complete with tripod, and my life list will take on a whole new perspective.

For now, my destiny is here. Each bird marks an indelible place in my heart. When I see a hawk fly overhead, I study the span of its wings and its ivory underbelly. I marvel at its ability to glide effortlessly with the wind, sunlight radiating through its feathers. As the hawk cries out, I wonder if it is a bird I know and if I have left an indelible mark in his heart as he has in mine.

I spread my arms wide and attempt to measure my own wingspan.

Emma Carter

Parker and I are in the kitchen cooking my birthday dinner and drinking a bottle of champagne. He is busy at the stove sautéing duck breast and appears to have everything under control. I watch as he gives the port wine sauce one last whisk, drops the asparagus into a pan of boiling water, and then lifts the lid on the wild rice to give it a stir.

Parker is a good cook; he is self-taught with the help of Julia Child's cooking shows from the 1960s. Frankly, when he cooks, there are few restaurants in town that I would choose over our own home.

I put the finishing touches on the green salads, topping each one with several nasturtium blossoms from our yard. Parker and I work in contented silence, each lost in our own thoughts. My favorite album by Steve Tyrell plays in the background. Argos watches, trying to decide which of us is the weaker link to food.

I turn to Parker. "Loraine and I have a bird release next Sunday. I keep forgetting to tell you. I made it for 1:00 in the hope you could come."

Parker inspects the flame under the duck pan. He is listening to me but talks to the stove. "I'll plan on meeting you there. I'm playing tennis with Mark in the morning, but I'll make sure we're done in time. Is it at the regular place?"

I lean against the counter and take a sip from my champagne flute. "Yeah, it's at the Meeker property."

"Are you ready to eat?" Parker turns off the stove and drains the asparagus into the sink.

"Yes, I'm ready."

Two plates garnished with parsley wait for the main course. Parker walks over to the fridge, takes out the bottle of champagne and refills my glass. Beautiful tiny bubbles rise to the surface. "Did your sister come by today?"

"Yeah, it was great to see her." I look at Parker and notice a scratch across his cheek.

"What's that?"

"What's what?"

"That scratch on your face."

Parker touches his cheek; his relaxed expression dissolves. He looks me straight in the eyes. "I had an altercation with a student."

"You had an 'altercation?' What does *that* mean?"

"A student slapped me across the face. She must have been wearing a ring."

"When were you going to tell me about this?" My voice comes out strained and tense. Parker and I have rules for disagreements: no sarcasm is rule number one. I come within molecules of violating our pact.

He winces. "I was hoping to get past your birthday."

"What happened?" I ask, trying to check my drama at the door.

"A grad student made a pass at me. I stopped her. She was insulted and slapped me."

I start to feel nauseated. Any appetite I once had is now gone. "What student? Do I know her?" I ask.

68

Parker looks at me and stalls. "I'd prefer not to say."

"You'd prefer not to say? I'd *prefer* that it had never happened," I respond with honesty, looking directly into his eyes.

"Me too."

I stand my ground, my feet planted firmly beneath me. I wait for the name.

"Lauren Cooper."

"Lauren Cooper? The Lauren Cooper who came to our house, who ate at our table? I think I'm gonna vomit."

"Luckily, Ed walked in and she left my office. It was perfect timing on his part. Lauren moves next week to Montana for her teaching position in Bozeman."

This is a recipe for a disastrous evening. What would Julia Child say? Sautéed duck breast served with a port wine sauce, infused with heartache and three tablespoons of anger. I once watched one of her shows where a whole chicken fell on the floor. Without missing a beat, she took a sip of wine and confessed to her audience that the guests would never know. Maybe Julia would have advice for saving my birthday dinner. Following her example, I take a swig of champagne.

Parker studies me to assess the damage. The phone rings, breaking the tense silence.

I suddenly feel bone tired. "Let's just let the machine pick up."

The phone rings four times before triggering our antique answering machine. We listen to our recorded greeting, and then my mother's voice bursts into the kitchen blaring like a trumpet. "Hi, Emma! Where are you? It's your mother. Happy birthday! Sorry I missed

69

you. You and Parker are probably out to a nice dinner. I hope Sarah brought over my gift for you. Call me when you have time. Parker, I hope you've stopped working so hard."

Just as the answering machine shuts off, the phone rings again. I expect this will be my mother, having forgotten to communicate a stray thought.

"Hey, Beautiful!" says Savannah in her southern drawl. "I know you two are screening calls. You're probably in the middle of dinner. Happy birthday *again,* Emma! I hope you've had a great day. Let's get the girls together for dinner when Parker is away in Boston. I love you! *Hey, I love you too, Parker, you handsome devil you!"*

I find myself breathing again. The phone functioned like the bell at a boxing match. It gave us time to retreat to our respective corners of the ring, take a sip of water, and have our brows dabbed with a cool white cotton towel.

Parker reaches for me and takes me in his arms. "I'm not going to let anyone or anything ruin your birthday, Emma."

Tears fill my eyes. "Thank you." I pause and take a breath. "I'm sorry about what happened with Lauren. Are you all right?"

"Yes, I'm all right." Parker says to me.

We linger in our embrace, looking into each other's eyes. A million unspoken words are acknowledged in that moment. Parker gives me a kiss on the lips.

I smile and say, "You'd better not overcook that duck."

"For you—*never!*" He walks back to the stove and resumes his cooking tasks. Parker returns the asparagus to the stove and reheats them with a quick butter sauté. With a few artful moves, dinner is up and going again.

I take a sip of champagne while I watch Parker. "So anyway, Sarah and I had a nice visit. She sends her love to you. She gave me a beautiful teacup for my birthday. It is quite exquisite. There is a Korean woman in the bottom of the cup. The impression of her face is actually imprinted within the porcelain."

Parker turns to look at me. "A Korean woman? That's pretty exact."

"Yeah, I put her in the china cabinet."

Parker starts to laugh as he puts dinner on the plates. "She should be safe there."

I smile at him. "I sure hope so. I locked the door."

I carry the salad plates into the dining room. Parker follows me, setting down his artfully arranged duck dinner. He strikes a match and cups his hand around the flame to light the waiting candles.

Once again, Parker strikes a match and cups his hand around the flame. This time he lights a small birthday candle sunk into a piece of chocolate cake. The dining room table reveals a memory: candles still burning, dirty dishes abandoned, and dinner napkins tossed to the side. We are in the living room sitting on the couch; the lit fireplace adds to the romantic glow. My mother's gift sits on the coffee table in front of me. Argos snores and kicks out his front legs, chasing rabbits in a dream.

With festive cheer he begins to sing, "Happy birthday to you…happy birthday to you…happy birthday dear Emma, happy birthday to you!"

I can't help but laugh out loud. Parker takes a fork and offers me the first bite of cake. I savor the flavor of bittersweet chocolate melting in my mouth.

"Do you want to open your mother's gift first?"

"All right," I say, wiping chocolate from the corners of my mouth.

My usual care in opening gifts seems to have gone by the wayside. With reckless abandon, I open the gift from my mother. She has given me a beautiful address book. The illustration on the cover is a map of the world. It appears old and sacred. In each of the four corners, a fruit tree depicts the seasons. The trees frame the map of the world through the limbs on the top while the roots anchor the bottom.

Parker is impressed. "That's really nice."

"It is. It's perfect," I say, surprised by my instant attraction to the gift.

My mother has good taste, but somehow this gift feels especially appropriate. I turn the pages, already excited about entering names, addresses, phone numbers, and emails. My current address book is old and not up to date. People have moved, changed names, and some have even died. In addition, it overflows with mementos that don't seem to have a home anywhere else, such as wedding announcements, stray photos, notes from friends and a recipe or two that never made it into the kitchen. My address book reveals the passing of time and the changes that life brings. In its own way, it's the history of my life: a collection of old lovers, friends, relatives, and new births. This address book is a timely gift from my mother, one that is long overdue.

Parker can tell I'm lost in reverie. He interrupts my silence. "Emma, are you ready for your gift from me?"

"Of course!" I say, returning my focus to him.

Parker gets up and leaves the room. He returns with a huge, colorfully wrapped gift and sets it in front of me. Despite the enormous size of the gift, he is able to lift it effortlessly. There is only one thing this could be—*luggage*. Remembering what the psychic said about "investing in good luggage," I am suddenly caught off guard by the gift. Parker doesn't notice my hesitation.

He sits down next to me. "This is something for the future. Something you have needed for a while. Something you have admired in the past and something that promises adventure."

Reluctantly, I untie the big bow and unwrap the gift. Sure enough, it is a full set of luggage, made from a beautiful tapestry fabric. Each bag has been placed inside another, like Russian nesting dolls. The psychic's predictions seem to be unfolding in front of me. I feel like I'm on a train moving toward some unknown destiny. Other than my new luggage, I'm completely unprepared for the journey. My knuckles turn white as I cling to my life as I know it.

Parker turns to me. "Do you remember when we were in New York last spring? A woman at the airport had this luggage, and you loved it. It took me a while to find it for you."

I do my best to convey enthusiasm. "Thank you for remembering and for all of your effort to make my birthday so special. The luggage is beautiful."

I pause and survey my surroundings. A fire in the hearth warms the living room, Argos sleeps peacefully, and my husband of nearly fifteen years sits beside me. Parker has gone to great lengths to find this meaningful gift. I have no idea what journey beckons, but I do know that I am fortunate to share a home and life with these two faithful companions. My heart fills with love and humble gratitude.

I lean back against the couch and then turn to Parker. "In the entire world, you're my favorite gift. You are priceless and irreplaceable. Thank you for sharing your life with me." My eyes fill with tears, and emotion lodges in my throat.

A warm smile crosses Parker's face. His eyes meet mine as he strokes my cheek with the back of his hand. I feel myself relax, give in, and surrender to the moment. Parker puts his right arm around my shoulders and turns his body into mine.

"Thank you, Emma," he says softly.

With his left hand, he takes a strand of my hair and puts it under his nose as if to savor a glass of French Montrachet. He looks into my eyes and smiles the smile that knows all my forbidden secrets. The energy shifts. I feel myself falling, my stomach lunging down. The truth is, my husband began his seduction this morning with his note by my teacup, the roses overflowing their vase, and the beautifully set table. It is a slow and deliberate web he weaves. I don't realize I'm being ensnared until the cumulative effect of his actions makes me melt and weaken. By the time his finger traces my eyebrow, slowly moves to my temple, and then outlines my chin—I'm completely undone. His fingers part my lips only to be replaced by the warmth of his mouth against mine. There is a profound intimacy about him—*about us.* He looks into my eyes and remains with me. I've never been able to resist him, never wanted to. My body longs for him, aches for him to be inside me. I am enraptured by his touch and lose all sense of place and time.

Emma Carter

For years, I have been teaching high school English. I teach Gate students, high achievers who excel academically. There are sixteen students in my senior Gate class this year. It is mid-April, and graduation is just around the corner. I have grown to love all of my students, but they will soon fly away from the nest to make their own way in the world. This is always a bittersweet time for me.

I teach the work of Joseph Campbell every spring. His work is fascinating and multicultural and can be used to analyze literature and events in contemporary culture. The hero's journey, which Campbell describes so well, in many ways will mirror my students own processes, challenges, and triumphs.

I turn to them and begin what will be one of my final teaching days with this group. "Joseph Campbell brought stories, myths, and traditions from other cultures to life. Many stories are archetypal. As we have learned, archetypal means that there are basic themes that link time and cultures. Examples are: the story of a baby in a basket floating down a river, the prince in search of his princess, or the tale of the hero. Through understanding the stories of others, we understand ourselves on a deeper level."

I pick up a piece of chalk and prepare to write on the board but pause and turn back to address my students. "Joseph Campbell identified three fundamental phases of the hero's journey." I pause, surveying my students, deciding whom I should call upon. "Simon, can you tell us the first phase and give an example?"

Simon looks at me and answers without hesitation. "The first phase is separation. The hero has to separate himself from normal life. The hero leaves home and goes on some sort of trip or journey. Like Bilbo Baggins in *The Hobbit.* He had to leave the comfort of the Shire." He stops talking, but I can tell he isn't finished. I've learned to wait for him, accepting his process, and so have the other students. He looks back up at me. "Sometimes there is resistance to go. Bilbo didn't feel ready or prepared for an adventure. It wasn't his idea to go anywhere. He liked the safe and predictable life of the Shire."

Simon's example hits a small but meaningful nerve as I think of my new luggage and my own resistance. I turn to the board and write the word *Separation.*

"Very good, Simon. Thank you. Deanna, how about phase two?"

Deanna doesn't like to be put on the spot. I sympathize as I watch her struggle against a straightjacket of shyness.

"Aaaahhh…Initiation. Initiation is phase two. There are lots of trials and tests, and they're hard. Like Odysseus, who traveled for years, fought off the Cyclops, had to deal with the Sirens, and got lost at sea. He did all that before he returned home."

I turn to the board and write the word *Initiation.*

"Great example Deanna, which sets us right up for phase three. Anyone?"

A few hands are raised. I point to Candice. Candice is a cheerleader whose blessed intelligence matches her beauty. I wrote her a letter of recommendation for college; she will be going to Berkeley for premed.

"Phase three is the return, after the heroes have gone through the hard stuff and survived. They learned their own strength and gained an understanding of their character. Like Lily in *The Secret Life of Bees*. She learned that family isn't always the people we're related to. Her home and family turned out to be with people from a whole different heritage."

I add the word *Return* to the list on the chalkboard.

"Excellent! Thank you, Candice. Those are three great examples. I'd like you to choose a book we have read this year: Homer's *Odyssey, The Hobbit, The Diary of Anne Frank*, or *The Secret Life of Bees*. Write a paper that analyzes a character through the lens of the hero. What is the call to adventure? What precipitates the separation? What happens during the hero's initiation, and what wisdom is gained? I want you to consider the symbolism in the stories. What does it mean to be on a grand adventure in unknown lands, versus being confined in a secret annex? How does environment impact the journey of the hero? What about the deep longing for home? Is the desire for home always part of the hero's experience?"

I begin to pace back and forth in the front of the classroom. I realize that I'm lost in my own thoughts of orphans. I stop and look at my students. "How do psychological wounds give characters substance? A wound creates an opportunity to heal; the scar becomes the memory that contributes to the development of identity. What are the wounds of these characters? How do their wounds enrich the story? Is there an aspect of the hero that is also an orphan? What does it mean to be lost or to lose our way?"

I look at the clock. The second hand moves rhythmically. Class is almost over. "Use short in-text quotes, long quotes, and a works cited page. I've typed the instructions for your assignment; please pick up a copy on your way out. One last thing: as all of you know, I volunteer with The Raptor Rehabilitation Center, and we will be doing a wild bird release this Sunday at 1:00 at the Meeker property just north of town. You are all welcome to come."

The bell rings. Students gather their books and belongings and exit the room. Simon approaches me with books in hand, backpack slung over his shoulder.

"What kinds of birds will you be releasing?" he asks.

"There will be a great horned owl, a red-tailed hawk, and possibly a falcon, if he is ready."

Simon is intrigued. "How do you know when they're ready?"

"When they successfully kill living prey."

Simon expected a different answer, and his surprise shows. He looks at me, head tilted to the side. "I'd like to bring my little brother. Would that be okay?"

I know all about Simon's brother. He suffers from depression. He can barely stay awake during school. The consensus among the teachers is that he is overmedicated.

80

I smile at Simon. "That would be great. I'll look forward to meeting him."

The last student to leave, Simon shuts the classroom door behind him. I am left surrounded by silence. I stand looking at the empty room and the abandoned desks. I know exactly who sits where. I feel a profound hollowness in my chest. This time of year is always difficult for me, and this one seems worse than usual.

I glance back at the chalkboard and am struck by how foreign my own handwriting looks: "Separation, Initiation, and Return."

Savannah Jones

♦

Not many African Americans in Santa Barbara. I certainly stand out in the crowd; we make-up a mere two percent of the population here. Latinos—now they are the largest minority, coming in at a healthy thirty-eight percent. Their presence colors the city with music, fabulous food, and Catholic churches. Every summer, Fiesta arrives with a twirl of colorful skirts, decorated horses, and flamenco guitarists. Thousands of people all dusted with confetti, walkin' on broken eggshells, line State Street to watch the parades.

I moved to Santa Barbara from South Carolina. I came to study with Cecile Watkin in UCSB's MFA program. My love is ceramics—ceramics that capture the experience of the South—specifically, the black South. Mostly, I create ceramic dolls. I clothe them in dresses and trousers made from old quilts. Sometimes I use patterned cotton from twenty-five pound sacks of White Lily Flour. I leave the flour embedded in the fabric. All dusted in white, the dolls look like biscuits fresh from the oven. My work has been shown in art galleries across the nation. I'm known for my provocative expression of slavery and the experience of the black American.

Now, I love Santa Barbara, but it does take some gettin' used to being around all these white folks. It's a given when I grocery shop at Lazy Meadows that I will be the token black. Today is no exception.

I approach the produce department, surprised to see my dear friend Emma. Her purse has the image of Toto on it and sits in the baby seat of the cart, just like a dog. She stands in front of the peach display, and I watch her selectively squeezing peaches, a cardinal sin throughout the country to hard-workin' farmers.

I pull my cart next to Emma's. "Don't you be bruisin' that good fruit, ya hear!"

Emma jumps outa her skin, turns to see me and begins to laugh. "Savannah! You scared me!"

"You deserve to be scared. Down South they'd have your head for that."

Emma steps over and embraces me. "Thank you for my birthday phone call," she says.

"You're welcome, darlin'." We exchange kisses, like women do.

I met Emma at UCSB. She was killin' time waiting on her husband. She came over to the art studios and began to wander the halls as if searching for somethin' unknown even to her. There I was, clay all over me, apron soaked and hair in thirty directions. No doubt about it, I looked just like one of my dolls. She became intrigued with my work, and conversation quickly ensued. Before I knew it, we were havin' lunch, and I was tellin' her my deepest dreams. That was four years ago, and I'm still here, still havin' lunch with Emma—still dreamin'.

I smile at her. "That was some birthday party. *Damn*...My romance is unfoldin' exactly like the psychic said it would. How amazin' is that! OOOOOWeeee...I've

84

never seen anythin' like it. That woman has a connection to God. *Where on earth did Roxanne find her?"*

Emma looks at me, her eyes roll and a sarcastic smile consumes her face. "Who knows? Probably in the Yellow Pages," she retorts.

My words come out bitin'. I'm not known for mincin' them. "The Yellow Pages? Emma–you don't find a woman like that in the Yellow Pages, *and you know it!* Somethin's up your ass, and I think it's called the TRUTH!"

I pause, lookin' at her, and I begin to question her integrity. "What ya' gonna do about that *Korean* brother of yours?"

Emma begins to laugh. "I haven't decided. I'm not sure I want to chase after something a psychic said."

"What are you so afraid of?"

"I'm not afraid of anything. But even if it is true, it was my father's story, not mine. Maybe some things are better left in the past."

"Why…I'm *disappointed* in you. I thought you had more *c h a r a c t e r* than that." Like a straight penetratin' arrow, this question of "character" deeply embeds itself into Emma's heart. I can see it, clear as day.

. "Why are you so invested in this?" Emma responds defensively.

"Cause I believe it, girlfriend. And I think you believe it too!"

Emma glares at me; she slits her eyes, actin' all mean. "Savannah, don't you have some ceramics in the kiln?" She appears to be entertained by her own cleverness.

"As a matter of fact, I do…And don't you have a life of denial callin'? Damn, it's callin' so loud even I can hear it. You go on now, you git. Git on back to that life of denial. But I'm not gonna lose my faith in you."

Emma begins to twist and turn, like a gator in a noose.

"I need to go," she says, actin' all high and mighty, like she is the Queen of Everythin'.

I look at her, and I know, deep in my heart, that this issue of her brother is not over. "Give my regards to that husband of yours."

"I will," she says with a pinch of lemon juice. Lord have mercy! She must need a ladder to get on that high horse of hers.

We each go our own way, smartin' from words.

As I'm selectin' a citrus body scrub, out of the corner of my eye I see Emma leavin' the store. I feel badly about our exchange. I run to the open doorway as she makes her way across the parkin' lot.

I call to her, "Emma! Emma!"

She turns to look at me.

With my best southern Baptist voice I yell, "Emma, I'm not gonna lose my faith in you!" People turn and look at me, then at Emma.

She is pissed. Without answerin', she turns away, both hands on the grocery cart, the wheels makin' a hell of a racket. Emma's hair flies out from behind her—there is no wind. She has the fury of the Wicked Witch of the West ridin' her bicycle through the air, and I'll be *damned* if she doesn't have Toto, too!

I watch as she opens the trunk of her Jeep. I am inspired! I see an Emma doll in my future, part Wicked Witch and part Dorothy, except for this doll—*the face*—it'll be Korean.

86

Emma Carter

Angrily, I unpack the grocery bags in the kitchen, as I mimic Savannah sarcastically. *"The truth is up your ass. Go on now git—git on back to your life of denial."* I re-enact the scene as though I myself am a black woman from the South. Argos has followed me into the kitchen and watches me with concern in his eyes. Absorbed in my own antics, I don't notice that Parker has also entered the kitchen.

"Honey, is something up your ass?" His voice is infused with humor.

I turn to look at him and respond in a Southern drawl. "According to Savannah Jones, the truth is up my ass and I'm livin' a life of denial!"

"Where did all this come from?"

"The psychic."

I'm disgusted with myself, disgusted that I'm so caught up with the ranting of a psychic. Somehow, with a deck of playing cards *that woman* managed to turn my life upside-down. I feel my emotions getting the best of me.

My eyes lock with Parker's. "The psychic said I have a brother in Korea that Dad left behind. Savannah believes it."

Parker leans against the kitchen counter as if to stabilize his own reaction.

"Do you believe it?

"I don't know what to believe."

Parker looks at me, his head tilted to one side. "Is this why we're going to have dinner with Suzanne and Bob at a Korean restaurant?"

"Yes, it is."

"And what do you hope to achieve by eating kimchi?"

I can't help but smile. "Well, maybe a culinary revelation."

Emma Carter

Our doorbell rings, announcing the arrival of our friends, Suzanne and Bob.

Argos races to the front door. His eyes are button bright, and his tail wags his body. I am always charmed by his exuberance in greeting people. As humans, we could take a lesson or two from our devoted pets.

Bob is a colleague of Parker's. Over the years, his wife, Suzanne, and I have become good friends as well. We don't socialize with them as often as we'd like. Time has a way of passing and weeks turn into months, but Suzanne and I keep in touch with periodic phone calls. Parker and Bob often have lunch together on campus.

Parker opens the front door, and we exchange boisterous greetings with our friends. Suzanne is a marathon runner and prides herself in having five percent body fat. I don't know where she finds the energy to exercise every day. Bob, on the other hand, is a heavy, big man. They always strike me as an unlikely couple.

Bob and Suzanne step into our house but linger at the doorway.

"Emma made a dinner reservation, but we could probably have a quick drink if you'd like," says Parker. It is clear from their behavior that they will decline the offer, but the question is a hospitable gesture.

Suzanne looks at Bob and gauges her reply. "We have a new sitter, so we need to be mindful of staying on time."

Bob piggybacks on his wife's comments. "I'm starving. I hardly had any lunch." He rubs his stomach to further his point.

"In that case, we're ready," replies Parker.

"Let's take two cars," suggests Suzanne. "That way we can leave if there are any problems at home."

"Good idea," Parker responds.

Their world is so different from ours. We don't have to consider the babysitter or backup plans. We could arrive home at five in the morning and Argos wouldn't even notice; chances are he would be snoring on the couch.

We leave a light on in the house. I grab my purse and a shawl.

Argos sits at the front door and watches our exit. I bend down and give him a kiss on the head. "You be a good boy and watch the house," I say to him.

Parker shuts and locks the front door.

Always a gentleman, Parker opens the restaurant door for us to walk through. Etched in the glass are the words: In-hwa Kim's Korean House of Blessings. As the door opens, a large metal bell that hangs on a ribbon bangs against the glass and rings loudly. All four of us step into the restaurant and stand in the entryway. Oddly enough, the bell continues to ring after the front door closes.

The restaurant is full, mostly with Asians. Many of the diners stop eating, distracted by the demands of the ringing bell. Round faces with dark, almond-shaped eyes look in our direction. Even the wait staff momentarily pauses. For a fleeting second, time seems suspended in space. Then the moment passes and the bell comes to a rest. Life resumes, eating continues, and conversation flows.

Suzanne turns to me, notably oblivious to the bell or the watchful customers. Her face fills with excitement. "We love this place! We've already been here two times."

"Why didn't you tell me? We could have gone somewhere else," I say to her.

"No, we were ready to come back. Besides, I'm guessing it will be one of your new favorite restaurants," Suzanne pauses before finishing. "It's always good to try something different, you know?"

This sounds all too familiar, "try something different." It reminds me of my birthday party and the good intentions of "fun." Anxiety begins to take hold. Even though I chose to come here, I feel my appetite wane. I look at Parker. We communicate wordlessly. Sensing my discomfort, he puts his hand on my back and rubs it affectionately. I appreciate the gesture and am grateful for the momentary refuge. I wrap my arm around his waist; he kisses my cheek.

Like bees hovering over a hive, the drone of a foreign language fills the air. I am struck by the multigenerational customers—babies, children, parents, and grandparents. The ambiance is more like a family reunion than diners unknown to each other. One family visits with another over a booth divider. Hands touch each other, smiles are exchanged, and children are adored.

The aroma of exotic cuisine fills the air and permeates my skin. I recognize the smell of garlic and chili, but there are other fragrances—foreign spices—that I don't know. I imagine the ingredients have traveled around the world to be served here, arriving as freeze-dried roots, colorful vegetables pickled in glass jars, dried herbs, and powdered spices. The aromas are intoxicating, and I begin to feel as if I'm in an altered state induced by an unknown narcotic.

From the back of the busy restaurant, an elderly Korean woman slowly approaches us. Her body sways from side to side as if each step holds the memory of hard physical labor. She wears an ornate floral hanbok but appears awkward in the formality of its confinement. As she comes closer, I find myself fascinated by her. Her presence exudes a dynamic mind that has far more energy than her body. Her face, although old, is also beautiful and tanned by the sun. Her sparkling eyes lock with mine. I sense a joyful happiness about her and am sure that laughter resides just behind her lips. She walks directly up to me, gently bows and says, in slightly broken English, "Welcome to In-hwa Kim's Korean House of Blessings. We so happy that you here."

Not knowing quite what to do, I bow back. "Thank you."

Her eyes shift to the rest of the group, and she bows to acknowledge their presence. "We so happy that you here," she repeats to the others.

Parker, Suzanne, and Bob bow to her.

Turning to the counter, she takes four laminated menus from the display. Then, leaning in toward me, she whispers, "I have special table for you in back of restaurant." She says this as if we are receiving preferential treatment that should remain confidential.

She turns, leading the way, before I can respond. With her back to us, I look at the others, and we exchange intrigued smiles.

We follow her through the restaurant, moving at her pace. The tables are set with decorated paper placemats. The food is served on white plastic dishes, and the tea is in metal, nonbreakable pots. The no-nononsense decor is common in Asian restaurants and is what I expected.

As we walk through the dining room, conversations stop and heads turn to watch us. Inquisitive gestures are made in our direction. Even a small infant seems captivated by our presence; his round face follows our passage through the aisle. His eyes meet mine. I can't help but stare back at him. His body twists in the high chair, and he strains to see where we are going. He raises his chubby arms into the air—toward me—as if wanting to be picked up. I turn away.

The elderly hostess leads us into a private alcove at the back of the restaurant. Heavy celadon velvet drapes hang at either side of the doorway, held back by large brass hooks. We step into the private room. I'm awed by the beauty of our table, which is stunningly set. All of us look at it, speechless with surprise. The table is round and of ample size for four people. There are no plastic plates here. Earthenware dishes rest at each place setting. The tablecloth is an old textile with clusters of purple plum blossoms scattered across a sky-blue background. To amplify the effect, a floral arrangement of plum blossoms sits in the center of the table. The twiggy branches shoot out in all directions and are laden with flowers. The blossoms appear poised for pollination as if longing to be

93

fondled by bumblebees. A few stray blossoms have fallen and are scattered across the table, as though a sudden gust of spring air blew through the room.

The elderly hostess closes the drapes, isolating us completely from the sights and sounds of the main dining room. With the drapes drawn, the room is shockingly quiet. I feel myself relax and settle into my body.

I turn to Parker and notice how handsome he looks. His blue eyes meet mine, and he smiles. He looks so young and innocent, so fresh and untouched by the world. I feel like I am falling in love with him all over again. I savor the moment.

I look at the hostess and realize that her hanbok matches the tablecloth. Perhaps she, too, blew in with the warm spring breeze.

"This is so beautiful," I say to her, trying to convey my appreciation.

"Please sit." She touches my arm and gestures to the table as though we are guests in her home. Each of us takes a seat. She passes out the cheaply laminated menus, which now seem out of place.

"May I bring drinks?" she asks. "We have tea, Korean beer, *makgeolli*, yogurt cocktails, sake, or *poricha*. We have Coco-Cola, too."

Parker looks to Bob and gestures that he should order.

"*Makgeolli* for the table," Bob says, then looks to Suzanne and I. "Do you want tea as well?"

Suzanne glances at me, and without waiting for a response, she replies, "Yes, we'll have tea."

The elderly woman nods, acknowledging the requests, then leaves the room.

I can't help but laugh at Bob. "You *are* a regular. *Makgeolli!* What is *makgeolli?*"

"It's a fermented rice drink. Evidently, it is quite popular in Korea."

A young man, smartly dressed in black, enters our private alcove. He places several small plates of food on our table, each artfully arranged. He points to the dishes and provides the name: "*Milssam, sang ho chi,* pickled daikon, and marinated beans sprouts."

I smile at him. "Thank you."

He bows and leaves the room.

"I think we're in for a real treat!" says Susan, clearly excited.

Parker turns to me and whispers into my ear, "Maybe even a culinary revelation."

I nod my head to acknowledge the comment.

Bob looks puzzled. "I guess the key is to make a reservation. We've always just walked in before."

Somehow I think there is more to this than just making a reservation.

The elderly woman returns with a platter of seafood: octopus, tiny squid, and clams, surrounded by seaweed. She sets the platter in the center of the table. The presentation is extraordinary.

She gestures to Bob. "You hungry. My treat to you."

"Fantastic!" says Bob as he reaches for a clam.

She gently bows, then leaves the room.

Parker helps himself to a piece of *milssam*, thin pancakes filled with strips of colorful vegetables.

The young male server arrives with the *makgeolli*. He pours the beverage, then leaves.

"To great friends!" offers Bob.

"To great friends!" we reply in unison, lifting our glasses to toast.

I take a sip of *makgeolli* and swallow the wrong way. I can't help but cough.

Parker looks at me, "Are you okay?"

I struggle to get the words out. "Yes," I say. "I just swallowed the wrong way."

It is one of those coughs that won't be suppressed and continues to force itself on me. Time after time my body lunges forward. Parker puts his hand on my shoulders. All conversation at the table stops. My words come out strained. "I'm going to go to the restroom. Be right back."

Parker Carter

"Will she be all right?" Bob asks me.

"If she doesn't come back in a few minutes, I'll go check on her."

Bob takes a sip of *makgeolli.* "So, what are you working on, Parker?"

"I'm managing two research grants right now. They're taking a fair amount of time." The elderly hostess returns to the table and bows. Her eyes meet mine. "Ready to order, or I come back when wife returns?"

When I look at Bob, he is clearly poised to begin. I remember his comment back at the house, about being "starving." I am reluctant to begin without Emma, but I feel some social pressure. Suzanne and Bob are less formal about these kinds of things. "I guess we could start. She'll be right back."

"Go ahead. I'm not ready yet," says Suzanne, as she studies the menu.

"We were here last week and tried the BBQ beef. It was quite good," Bob says to the elderly woman.

"*Pulgoki,*" she says with emphasized enunciation.

Bob repeats, "*Pulgoki.* Yes, I'll have that."

She turns to me next.

"What do you recommend?" I ask her.

Her eyes bore into mine. I get the distinct impression she is doing more than assisting me with my dinner order. Her face etches itself into my memory.

"For you, *samgyeopsal*, grilled pork belly," she says as if a light bulb of truth just went on.

I nod to her. "Okay, that sounds great. Thank you."

The elderly hostess looks at Suzanne, who clearly expects the same assistance. Without hesitation, the elderly woman responds, "*Sundubu jjigae*, tofu soup with vegetables."

Suzanne's face lights up. "Perfect!"

Emma returns to the table, no longer coughing. I reach over and pull out her chair. She sits and quickly opens her menu.

In-sook Lee

I am dead now. My sister, Min-sook, is a shaman. Through her, we are both here tonight. I am an ancestor who is time traveling. I have chosen the age when I was happiest. I am twenty-five years old and in love with Emma's father. His baby, so small, lives inside of me. My sister, still living, is her current age of eighty-one.

I step inside the private dining room with a pot of green tea. The tea leaves have been steeped in love and unspoken history. I have stirred the leaves, blending the flavor, imagining the past infused with the present.

Emma looks like her father. His gestures live in her movements. I feel both joy and profound sadness.

Years ago, Randall showed me a wedding photo of Emma and Parker. Their faces glowed with the happiness of new lovers. They were like plum blossoms greeting spring. Randall and I were once plum blossoms, too.

I am trying to make peace with my past—with the disappointments that transpired during my life. My hope relies on Emma. She is the chosen one. It is through her that my past—and her future—can be healed for both the living and the dead.

Emma Carter

♦

As I sit down, a young woman comes to the table. I haven't seen her before. She is dressed in a crisply ironed, navy hanbok. She is astonishingly beautiful. Her hair is flawlessly arranged in a tight bun, which only accentuates her perfect skin and deep brown eyes. She pours tea for me and then sets the pot on the table. Although Suzanne was the one who ordered the tea, it wasn't poured for her, and she seems to have lost interest in drinking it.

I feel out of sync with everyone else at the table. Their menus are folded; it is obvious that they have ordered. I suppress a twinge of irritation, remembering that Bob was starving and probably wanted to order. Suzanne holds a photo album in her hands and animatedly talks about the pictures as she points to the images.

I look up at the waitress. Feeling rushed to order, I hold the menu and point to a colored photo of skewered chicken with vegetables. I must admit, the photo looks dubious, even to me.

"How about this?" I ask.

"This dish is too plain for you. It lacks *c h a r a c t e r.*"

I stare at her, taken back by her choice of words. I quickly glance at the others; they are oblivious to this exchange and remain deep in conversation.

The young Korean woman gently caresses her stomach. Although no pregnancy shows, it is a distinct maternal gesture that suggests an unborn child. She smiles at me. Her eyes trace my face like a painter with a brush in hand. Silence lingers between us.

Her eyes meet mine. "Tonight we have a family chef here from South Korea. His specialty is *mae un tang*, which is a hot and spicy fish stew. I recommend it for you. You need more water—less land. Poultry is land meat."

I find her comment odd and slightly offensive. What does it mean to "need more water?" I look at her. There is something familiar about her—the shape of her face, her nose and lips. I feel as if I have seen her—or know her.

"Have we met before?" I ask.

"No, we have never met."

I smile. "You sound so sure."

She bows to me. "I am sure. My name is In-sook."

"It's nice to meet you, In-sook."

I *have* seen her before. Maybe we have never met, but I know her face. Perhaps I've seen her on campus while visiting Parker.

"On your recommendation, I'll try the fish stew. Thank you."

In-sook bows and leaves the table. I feel unnerved by the waitress and detached from the group—maybe it's the *makgeolli*. The whole experience of this dinner seems otherworldly. The synchronicities of Korea are mounting. I take a sip of tea and watch Suzanne, Bob, and Parker. I am a witness instead of a participant at the table. Suzanne points to photos as she talks to Parker. Bob elaborates on his wife's conversation.

I watch Bob's lips move but don't hear a word he is saying. He catches my eye, and I smile at him. During the few minutes that I was talking to the waitress, Suzanne has almost finished showing the photos. I feel as though I slipped through a time warp while ordering my dinner.

Suzanne looks at me, flips back a few photos and then hands the group of snapshots to me. "Emma, just look at Bob. This is the funniest picture! Look at the other photos too. There are some great ones of the kids."

I make a sincere attempt to re-engage with our friends. I look at the photo of Bob. He holds a big rubber duck.

"Oh, that is funny!" I say.

Under the table, Parker puts his hand on my thigh. It must be obvious that I'm distracted. I turn to him and smile.

Suzanne takes a sip of *makgeolli*. "How about you guys? Do you have any exciting plans coming up?"

"I'm going to Boston for the American Psychological Association Convention," replies Parker. He looks at me. "Emma will be off for summer fairly soon. We haven't made any vacation plans yet."

Our conversation is interrupted by the arrival of food. Both Suzanne and I attempt to clear an open space on the table.

"Well, that's the fastest dinner I've ever been served at a restaurant!" says Bob.

The elderly Korean woman twinkles. "You hungry. I told chef hurry."

A busboy assists in serving the food, which is beautifully presented. The steaming bowl of s*ndubu jjigae* is set before Suzanne. The sautéed broccoli and snow peas are a brilliant green, the yellow squash looks divinely fresh, and red peppers accent the dish. The presentation is so vibrantly colorful that it looks more like a piece of art.

In-sook places the fish stew before me. The stew is full of vegetables, chunks of whitefish, lobster claws, and is topped with tiny squid. Steam comes off the bowl and swirls around my face. The complexity of aroma puts me into a state of deep relaxation.

The *samgyeopsal*, grilled pork belly, is put before Parker. Slices of pork rest atop a mountain of hot cabbage. The plate is garnished with julienned scallions and carved radishes and is sprinkled with sesame seeds.

Bob's hefty dinner looks equally delicious with an abundant pile of beef on cabbage. The fragrance of Bob's BBQ drifts over the table, captivating us all.

The artistry of this dinner reminds me of a *Gourmet* magazine cover from years ago. The authentic earthenware plates, the colorful vegetables, and the aroma are more than any of us expected.

The elderly Korean woman stands next to me and puts her hand on my shoulder. "Please eat—enjoy!" She then bows to the table and leaves the room.

Bob looks amazed. "It was good last time, but it sure didn't look like this."

The hospitality extended to us at this restaurant is more kindness than I've experienced at most family reunions. All four of us are silent as we begin to eat. Our facial expressions say it all. This is truly a divine culinary experience. *Memorable.*

Suzanne looks like she is in love. "This is the best dinner I've ever had. It's almost like she knew I was a vegetarian. Would anyone like to try my soup?"

Bob takes a spoonful of his wife's soup. He sits back in his chair reveling in contentment, savoring the mouthful. He swallows and then tilts his head back. "That is good! The flavors are so different, so complex," he says as if talking to himself. Bob then winks at Suzanne while licking his lips. It is a private, shockingly sexual exchange, one that wasn't meant to be seen by others. Evidently, I have underestimated him all these years. I feel awkward, as if I were an accidental voyeur. Suzanne looks at me, sensing that I witnessed the private exchange. She lets out a schoolgirl giggle.

I refocus on my own meal. "Would anyone like to try the fish stew?" I offer.

"I'd love to try some," says Bob.

Just as he is lifting his spoon and poised to take his sample, In-sook walks up and places herself between Bob and me. She completely stops our interaction. Bob retracts his spoon. In-sook reaches for the pot of tea and refills my cup. She positions her back toward Bob, blocking my view of him.

"How is the *mae un tang*?" she asks.

I smile at her. "It's fantastic. Thank you for your recommendation."

In-sook returns the smile, bows, and walks away.

"Bob, did you want to try some soup?" I ask.

Bob rubs his belly. He didn't seem to notice the interruption from the waitress. He has eaten almost all of his dinner.

"No, thank you. I think I'm too full." His face beams with joy.

I look at my bowl, now nearly empty, and wonder *how could I have eaten so much?* I lift my dish to get a final spoonful of broth. In fact, all of us are in the process of finishing every last bite from our plates. No one is talking, only eating. Even the oysters are all gone. It's as if we've fallen under a spell. Parker never eats everything on his plate, but tonight is an exception.

Suzanne takes her last bite, sets down her spoon, looks up, and smiles. She casually looks at her watch. Her surprise is evident. "It's almost nine-thirty! We've been here three hours. Where did the time go? We need to leave." She looks at Bob. "We're already later than we said we would be."

"We certainly enjoyed this restaurant," I say to her.

The waiter comes into the room and begins to clear away the plates.

"Could we get the check?" Bob asks him. The waiter nods in response.

Parker looks at Bob and Suzanne. "What a great dinner!"

Within seconds, the elderly hostess returns with the bill on a plate. Bob and Parker both reach for their wallets. Parker takes a look at the bill, and each of the men hand a credit card to the hostess.

Parker looks at her. "Could you please split this on the two cards?"

"Certainly," she says and leaves with the credit cards.

"That's the most reasonable dinner we've eaten," Parker says as he watches Bob yawn and stretch.

"How much was it?"

"It was only \$54.00."

"That can't be right," Suzanne says in exasperation.

"It was. Everything was on it."

I look at Parker. "Well, we need to leave her a good tip."

"Yes, I will." He looks at me, nodding his head in agreement.

The elderly Korean woman returns and hands the credit cards and receipts to each rightful owner, as if she knows exactly who is who.

"The dinner was wonderful. Thank you," I say to her.

She looks deeply into my eyes. "You welcome. Glad you enjoy flavor of Korea. Maybe we see you again."

Her authenticity is so unexpected and rare. I look at her and smile. "You will absolutely see us again!"

Her face illuminates. "We look forward to that." She gently bows and leaves.

I watch Parker as he signs the bill. He writes in a \$20 tip. I smile at him.

In unison, the four of us stand up to leave. I pick up my shawl from the back of my chair and sling my purse over my shoulder. Bob parts the heavy drapes. The dining room is now empty and silent. The families are gone, the children and the babies longing to be held. The still room is a bit of a shock. We were oblivious to the passage of time and to the other diners while in our own private corner. The tables have been cleared and re-set in preparation for tomorrow's lunch.

We walk through the quiet dining room. The elderly Korean woman waits at the front door.

"Thank you for coming. Thank you for coming," she says, bowing repeatedly.

I bow in return. "Thank you."

Parker opens the restaurant door. The once demanding bell now hangs silent.

Much to our surprise, it is raining outside. This is a radical change in the weather. The last I heard, the weekend was predicted to be sunny with temperatures in the mid-seventies.

We say goodbye to Bob and Suzanne. Hugs and kisses are exchanged as we huddle under the awning of Inhwa Kim's Korean House of Blessings.

The rain shows no sign of abating. Parker takes my hand, and we make a mad dash to our car. By the time we reach it, we are both soaked. The cold shower seems to have broken the restaurant's spell, and I feel more like myself. Once in the passenger's seat, I wipe the rain from my face.

I turn to Parker as he starts the engine. "Our waitress was unusual, don't you think?"

"What do you mean?"

"Did you hear what she said to me about my selection?"

Parker backs the car out and answers me with his head turned, looking out the rear window. "No, I was talking with Bob."

"She said I shouldn't order the poultry because I need more water in my body and less land." I pause, analyzing her statement. "I think that was her way of telling me I need to be more flexible."

Parker smiles as if silently agreeing. "I'm sorry I missed that."

"The whole experience felt very synchronistic."

Parker pulls onto State Street. "Synchronistic because of what the psychic said and because of the Korean woman in the bottom of your teacup that you locked in our china cabinet?"

This is why I love my husband. I assume he's not listening to me, and then it turns out he remembers something I said—that I myself had completely forgotten.

"Exactly," I respond. Now I'm the one who's smiling. "I think dinner was the culinary revelation I was hoping for, but I can't tell you why, because I don't understand why. It just feels like more information, like I'm in the midst of some sort of labyrinth and I'm trying to find my way with all the clues. I'm trying to understand the difference between my father's responsibilities and mine. It's not clear to me yet. I think I just need to be open to what shows up."

Parker reaches over and grabs my hand to give it a squeeze. Although he says nothing, his sense of understanding is relayed in that simple gesture. The rain beats down on the windshield. Visibility is poor. The wipers go back and forth in a synchronized rhythm. We drive in silence. I reach over and turn on the radio.

The DJ's sultry lounge voice fills the car. "Here's a classic song, *Chinese Café*, for all you Joni Mitchell fans. By the way, where did that rain come from?"

When I was young I had every Joni Mitchell album she recorded. Her voice filled the nooks and crannies of my bedroom while I was in high school. Later, her music billowed out the windows of my college apartment.

Years ago, album covers were works of art. Miniature CD covers just don't have the same impact vinyl covers once did. Now with technology, cyberspace has claimed the visual representation of music. My favorite album cover of Joni Mitchell's was *The Hissing of Summer Lawns*. The album cover is green with a backdrop of skyscrapers contrasted with natives carrying a huge anaconda through tall grass. The cover captures an image of colliding worlds, the modern world and the indigenous world, brought together by the snake. To this day, that particular album cover remains clear in my mind.

Music fills the car. I reach over and turn up the volume. This song takes me back to my senior year in college. I wore this album out: *Wild Things Run Fast*. Like an old friend who has stopped by to visit, Joni's voice is a welcomed companion. The words to the song come back to me as they are sung. I am struck by the irony of the lyrics. Now that I'm "middle aged" this song takes on a new meaning. Perhaps I, too, am caught in the middle, living in two worlds—one of reality, the other of avoidance. I think of my father and all the years we spent as strangers. So much lost time and barren memories.

If there is a Korean brother, he and I are strangers, too. Within a single family, a legacy of unspoken truth is honored between blood. I, also, have played a part, content to let silence reign.

I reflect on my father's love for a Korean woman, the psychic's story, the teacup from my sister, my new luggage, the unexpected poignancy of Joseph Campbell's *Hero's Journey*, and now the Korean restaurant.

I turn to Parker. "I'm going to start to call this the Ancestors' Conspiracy."

He answers me, as if reading my mind. "And before long, I'm going to believe you."

I crawl into bed, exhausted by the events of the day and full from too much food. I prop the pillows behind my head. The bed feels warm and comfortable, and a fluffy down comforter surrounds me. The bedside lamp casts a golden glow in the bedroom. I take my novel off the nightstand, put on my reading glasses, and open the book to find the words that were left behind yesterday. Regardless of my desire to sail around the world with Tania Aebi in *Maiden Voyage*, my head grows heavy and then nods to the side. I jerk it back upright. The book is too weighty for me to hold open. The pages want to turn inward. My hands can no longer support the image of the endless sea with its rhythmic swells.

My head falls to one side and sleep claims me. The dream world demands a presence:

I'm in a large, empty house. There are highly polished wood floors, and big, curtainless windows fill the room with light. It feels like an old colonial home. I sit in the middle of the living room weaving a tapestry. I wear an elaborate wedding dress. Yards of white satin consume the floor around me.

The tapestry is the same image from the cover of the address book that my mother gave me. I am weaving a map of the world with the seasons depicted by a tree. The tapestry is half done, which I understand to be symbolic of my life. Just as I'm about to use the golden-amber thread for the image of fall in the lower left corner, there is a knock on the door. I ignore it. The knock comes again, this time much louder. I am aware of the visitor but refuse to stop what I am doing. I want to continue to weave my life undisturbed.

Suddenly I notice In-sook, the young waitress from the restaurant, looking through the window at me. I'm not overly surprised to see her. It's as if I have been expecting her. In-sook's clothes are identical to what she wore last night at the restaurant—a navy blue hanbok. Her hair is arranged in a tight bun.

I look at her and our eyes meet. My attention returns to my tapestry. The next knock is more demanding. My father joins In-sook, and together they peer in the window. They are surrounded by many Korean children, of all different ages. The children call my name and laugh as they begin to pound on the front door. The presence of so many can no longer be ignored.

I stand up in full wedding regalia. The skirt of my wedding dress surrounds me, and the beautiful white satin shifts with my movements. My anxiety rises. I want to flee the pressures of their demands. I turn to look at the back of the house. The hallway is very, very long and resembles a hallway at an enormous Vegas hotel. At the end of the hallway is light and what appears to be blue sky.

I turn toward the back of the house and run down the hallway, my wedding dress flowing, floating ten feet behind me. I run as fast as I can, but it feels as if I'm running in slow motion. I run from my father, from In-sook, and from fear of all those children with their unmet needs.

The front door can no longer withstand the pounding and pressure. The door bursts open. The children swarm into the house, and in their enthusiasm they knock over my tapestry on its frame. The yarn and threads go flying. The children, in their colorful clothes, are happy and laugh as they chase me down the hall. There are hundreds of them. Their arms reach for me.

Finally, I get to the end of the hallway. The open doorway is at the top of a high cliff. Below me lies a rugged coastline. The ocean is large and expansive, and the waves crash to shore. It is a cloudless day. The blue sky meets the horizon of the ocean, and the sun's reflection scatters diamonds onto the water's surface.

I look back as the children rapidly approach. I have only seconds to decide. My feet inch up to the edge of the threshold. I stretch out my arms, parallel to the earth.

My eyes are completely focused. With one bounce, I form a perfect swan dive to the rocks below. I hear the billowing fabric of my wedding dress rustle through the air. I feel my dress transform and disappear.

I no longer dive to the earth and instead fly just above the shoreline. My arms are white wings, held straight out from my sides. My legs are bare and in alignment with my body, and my toes are pointed. I am now a white crane. The wind supports my body; the air rushes through my feathers. I can see for miles. The ocean's fresh air caresses my face. I feel elated and liberated.

I look back over my wing and am stunned to see thousands of white cranes flying in formation behind me. They extend as far as I can see.

I hear the sound of ocean waves crashing to shore. I reach over and turn off my alarm clock. The details of the dream are vivid in my mind. I turn over in bed. Parker lies next to me, still asleep with his arm thrown over his face as if to keep the light away. His shallow breathing contains a gentle snore.

"Honey? Are you awake?" I ask, knowing that he isn't. "Honey, wake up, I have to talk to you," I say more urgently.

He swims up from the depths of a deep sleep. He surfaces, pleading, "Can't it wait?"

"No–something has happened," I whisper to him. "I had a dream."

"You and Martin Luther King."

"No, honey, I need to tell you about it—really." My voice conveys urgency.

Parker surrenders. He doesn't open his eyes but moves over closer to me and puts his arm around me. I snuggle next to him, wrapping my legs around him.

"I'm listening," he says.

"That beautiful young waitress. I think she drugged us," I say, confessing my private thoughts of conspiracy.

Parker begins to laugh. *"You woke me up for that?* Emma, there was no beautiful young waitress. Do you mean the seventy-five–year-old?"

"No, *our waitress!"*

"She was our waitress."

My impatience grows. "Darling, what table were you sitting at? The twenty-five–year-old waitress wearing a navy blue hanbok."

"There was no twenty-five–year-old waitress in a navy blue hanbok."

"Are you trying to tell me our waitress was the hostess who greeted us at the front door—no other waitress?" I begin to feel queasy.

"That's right." Parker's eyes are now open, and he looks at me.

My head starts to spin. "I think I'm going to be sick."

Throwing off the covers, I run to the bathroom. I lift the toilet lid and bend over the bowl: nothing comes. My stomach churns, and I feel nauseated. I go to the sink and splash cold water on my face. I look at myself in the mirror, attempting to evaluate my own stability. Nothing has changed—*everything has changed*. I realize that trying to be open to the clues truly pushes me to the brink of my comfort zone.

Parker comes into the bathroom dressed in his boxer shorts. "Are you okay?" he asks, his voice filled with concern.

"No, I'm not okay," I reply emphatically. "Our waitress was around twenty-five years old. She said her name is In-sook." I look at him squarely. "You must have seen her!" I step over to him and take his face in my hands, preventing him from looking anywhere but at me. "Tell me!"

"No. I never saw the woman you're talking about. Let's go lay down, and you can tell me about your dream."

I follow him back to bed, and we stiffly lay in each other's arms.

"There was a woman, and her name is In-sook," I say, trying to convince him. "She rubbed her stomach as she told me what to order. I ate what she suggested. She said I needed more water and less land. She poured my tea. I have seen her before. I know I have."

"Where have you seen her?" Parker begins to sound concerned.

"I don't know. I thought maybe the University. I know her face. She said we had never met. She seemed sure of it."

"Emma, you have gotten yourself all worked up. It's entirely possible I just didn't see her."

"You would have seen her," I reply, knowing this is so.

"Well, maybe not. I was busy looking at photos and talking with Suzanne and Bob. I'm sure there is a reasonable explanation for all this. Turn over, and I'll rub your back for you."

I surrender and turn over. Parker lifts my pajama top. His warm hand caresses my skin. I take a deep breath and try to relax my body and quiet my mind. I focus on the moment: the blankets are warm, the bed is comfortable, and I feel Parker's body next to mine.

"Everything is okay," I say to myself, as I try very hard to convince myself that this is true. I struggle to find my internal ground. "Really. Really, everything is just fine. There is a reasonable explanation for all this."

I focus on Parker's warm hand rubbing my back.

Argos lies on the floor next to me, watching my every move. He lifts his head; his large brown eyes convey his devotion. I am reminded of Amber's reading and her referring to him as an "extraordinary companion." I remember Sarah and I laughing at this, thinking that it was way too obvious, but as I look into his eyes, I think Amber is right. He is extraordinary. There is something sacred about his presence. He is a gift in my life. His transparent compassion is palpable—and on this day—I am humbled by his love and commitment to me.

Argos, the Dog

I lie on the bedroom area rug and watch Emma and Parker. Usually Emma gets up first. Most mornings I follow her into the bathroom, she pets me, and our eyes linger. This is when I receive my first kiss of the day, smack-dab on the middle of my head. I guess my kiss this morning will have to wait. Although they went back to sleep, voices were raised and emotions flared. I felt the tension as though it were my own.

I notice movement on the bed, and I raise my head to watch Parker as he delicately removes himself from Emma's slumbering hold. He slides his feet into his slippers next to the bed and then quietly puts on his robe. He gestures for me to get up, and we both exit the room. He slowly shuts the door behind us.

We go down the stairs together. I'm an old dog now, so I waddle behind him, struggling to keep my balance. This is my favorite time of day. The house is peaceful, and of course, this is when I get my morning ration of food.

With arthritic enthusiasm, I follow Parker through the living room and into the kitchen. Parker walks to the pantry and gets a scoop of kibble. Anticipatory drool drips from the side of my mouth. He fills my ornamental bowl that reads "Lucky Dog" and sets it onto the floor. I put my face down into the bowl and inhale. I'm so distracted by the chicken-and-rice flavor (my favorite, although beef and barley runs a close second) that I don't realize Parker has picked up the phone. He is already in the middle of a conversation when I look up and lick my lips.

"What a great dinner last night. Did your sitter work out okay?" Parker asks.

"That's good. Yes, of course," I hear him say.

My focus returns to my empty bowl; I compulsively lick it, hoping for an essence of lingering flavor. My dog tags clink against the side of the bowl. It's no use; the food is all gone. I sigh and sit down.

My full attention now goes to Parker. "There are some good movies out. I thought maybe we could get together next week for a guys' night out," he says.

Parker pauses and looks at me. My forepaws slide down on the kitchen tile. I now eavesdrop from a reclining position. Eavesdropping is one of my life's missions; it is a full-time job for me: the words, the tone of voice, and the intensity of the conversation are all of paramount importance. I also track the comings and goings of Emma and Parker. In addition, I survey the parameters of both the house and the yard. I take great pride in my responsibilities as a dog. I always have.

"That would be fine." Parker hesitates. "I know this is an odd question—our waitress last night—how old do you think she was?"

As I watch Parker, Emma enters the kitchen. She looks disheveled: her hair is uncombed and her robe hangs open. She quietly sits down on a bar stool, and she, too, watches Parker.

Parker listens to the voice on the other end of the phone. He nods his head as he looks out the window. "Yes, it must be difficult to work so hard at seventy-five."

Parker turns and sees Emma. She surprises him, but her presence does not deter his investigation. "Bob, did you see a young waitress come to our table, someone in her mid-twenties?"

My eyes dart back and forth between Emma and Parker. Something important is happening, although I don't completely understand it. Parker nods his head as he listens.

"That sounds great. See you next Wednesday at the River Theatre." He sets down the phone and looks at Emma.

Emma puts her elbows on the counter and rests her chin in her hands. "What's the verdict?" she asks.

"There was only one waitress: seventy-five years old, but they'd never seen her before. Bob did say that dinner last night far exceeded their past experiences. He and Suzanne were just talking about it."

Parker takes the kettle and fills it with water. "How about some tea?"

"All right," she says, looking a bit unraveled.

Emma looks at me, and her eyes fill with tears. It pains me to see her in such sadness. I struggle to get up off the tile floor, but my paws slip on the smooth surface. After repeated attempts I am able to stabilize myself. I go to Emma, wanting to comfort her. I rest my head on her thigh and gaze into her watery brown eyes. She gently strokes my ear. "The woman in the restaurant was my father's lover from Korea—a ghost." With her eyes never

121

leaving mine, she unloads her heavy heart. "In my dream she was with my father, wearing the same exact clothes she wore last night. There were many Korean children in the dream. They were chasing me, and I was running from them."

"A ghost?" Parker asks in bewilderment. "That's not the answer I was expecting."

She bends over and kisses my head. Our beloved ritual is late but not forgotten.

"Are you going to be all right?" Parker says to Emma.

"Yeah, I'm going to be all right," she says, not very convincingly.

The kettle whistle blows. Parker makes tea and sets out two cups and saucers.

"How about some eggs and toast?" he asks.

"I don't want to eat. I feel sick."

Parker pulls out a frying pan, and takes butter and eggs from the fridge and a loaf of bread from the bread drawer. He slices two pieces of bread and puts them into the toaster.

"An empty stomach won't help. I'll make breakfast, and you eat what you can." Parker picks up a knife and cuts off a chunk of butter, adding it to the pan while lighting the flame. He looks over at Emma. "I'm getting the distinct impression you believe this. Do you really think your dad left behind a woman and child?"

"Why wouldn't I? My father abandoned my sister and me, and we're not half Korean."

I understand now. Emma will find this intolerable. Her previous lifetime will begin to haunt her: her pregnancy, Parker leaving her, her grief over his death, and the most grueling of all, allowing their baby to die. Let me be clear. I have never held the death of the baby against Emma. She did what she had to do. Emma was a victim of social and historical ignorance. It's as simple as that.

We all stand in the kitchen, Emma and Parker completely unaware of the significance of this karmic moment. Humans are very interesting. They are surprisingly naive. They don't understand that the seeds planted in one lifetime lead to the fruits or the decay in the next.

Butter sizzles. Parker cracks the eggs into the pan: one, two, three, and four. I make eye contact with him and begin a demanding howl. Parker then cracks a fifth egg into the pan. I know this last egg is for me. As though on automatic drip, saliva fills my mouth.

Emma pauses, leans over, and inspects my identification tags as if contemplating ownership.

Her focus returns to Parker. "Do I believe he was capable of turning his back on responsibilities *he literally created*? Absolutely. I'm living proof."

"Is there any evidence that this could be true?"

"I have one photo of the Korean woman he was involved with there. I have one of his old résumés that lists his military positions, with international locations. It might be helpful in pinpointing a location in Korea."

Parker stops cooking and looks at Emma. "I don't remember the photo."

"I retrieved it from his things, after he died. I'm sure I showed it to you. The woman is in a slip; her arms are over her head. My dad's foot is in the corner of the photo."

"Where is it?"

"Who knows? I haven't seen it since we moved two years ago. It's somewhere in the garage—and you know what our garage looks like. I wouldn't know where to begin looking."

"Why'd you take it?" he asks, puzzled.

"Because my father treasured it. If it were thrown away, it would somehow erase the past. I felt obligated to honor the photo of her—for him. It survived through his four wives, and now it survives his death."

"Did your dad ever talk about this woman?" Parker pours Emma a cup of tea and hands it to her.

"Yeah, he did. He met her when he first arrived in Korea. She was his interpreter. I believe he remained in love with her throughout his entire life."

"Have you told Sarah about this?"

"No," says Emma, as she ties her robe and tries to pull herself together.

"Why not?"

Emma responds in a dramatic southern drawl, *"Because I'm livin' a life of denial."* She sounds just like her friend Savannah.

I smell something burning and begin to growl. I wave my nose through the air, in circle-eight formation, trying to detect exactly what it is. Smoke rises from the toaster.

"Shit!" says Parker, as he lifts the toaster lever and unplugs it. He fishes the charred bread out with a knife. He then lowers the flame under the eggs.

Emma leaves her cup of tea and opens the kitchen window to let in fresh air.

Parker rinses off the toast as I watch from beside the sink. I inspect the burnt bread. He takes the charred toast over to the trash can, opens the can lid with the foot step, and then throws it away. What a waste.

Emma shakes her head, disgusted and angry. "I resent this," she says as she takes silverware out of the drawer. "Sometimes there is a fine line between deep inner knowing and delusional thinking. At this moment, I'm not sure which side of the line I'm on," she says with a fistful of cutlery. Emma steps over to the countertop and sets down the silverware. She turns, looks at Parker and says, "You appear to be neutral about all this."

Parker slices two new pieces of bread. "I think it's far-fetched. Is this something you could talk about with your mother on the phone, or do you need to wait and do it in person?" He pops the bread into the toaster and then raises the flame on the stove.

"Over the phone is fine. They've been divorced for forty years. At this point, there isn't much about my father that would surprise her."

"Then I think you should talk to her about it. Let's see if she thinks there is any validity to the story."

Emma opens another drawer, takes out two placemats and napkins and proceeds to set the countertop for breakfast. The morning paper lays rolled up, secured with a rubber band. As Emma slips it off, she sighs. "I wish I didn't have that bird release today."

"Maybe it's a good thing," Parker says as he flips the eggs.

"Yeah, maybe it is."

I begin to howl in rebellion. We're no longer in the middle ages. My egg isn't getting any fresher, and I'm not getting any younger. Parker looks at me, the same look

125

I've seen for many lifetimes. "Getting a little anxious, are we?" he asks, his voice lilting with a subtle Scottish accent. And in that precise moment in time, I am back in Skye, and he and I stand looking out to sea, contemplating the depths of the unknown.

Emma Carter

I'm still unnerved by my morning and am undoubtedly quieter than usual. Loraine sits in the passenger seat in my Jeep. The two crated birds are in the back. We hear them struggle to find stability in the moving car. I am empathetic.

"Brandon Locke from the newspaper will be meeting us at the release site to do a story about the birds," Loraine says, looking out the window, as if speaking to the landscape.

"That's great. We could use some press. Perhaps it'll help us get more volunteers."

Silence fills the car and presses against my chest. I crack the car window to breathe. Loraine turns to me. "Something is up with you, Emma. You're not yourself. Is everything all right?"

It is difficult to know what to say. On one hand it would be liberating to discuss my father and prospective brother. On the other hand, the less said the better. I stop at a red light and turn to face Loraine. "Have you ever heard of that old saying, 'He who does not heed the call gets dragged'? I'm in the process of being dragged. The sick irony of this is that I'm teaching Joseph Campbell right now, *The Hero's Journey*."

The light turns green and once again we are westbound. "I'm on my own hero's journey Loraine. Phase one to be precise." I pause to focus on passing a car. "To use my student's example, I'm like Bilbo Baggins. Our Shire is very comfortable. I like my routine; it's safe and predictable. I'm not sure if I want to leave home. I've worked very hard to get my life exactly as it is."

Loraine looks at me and her face fills with compassion as she dissects the riddle. "Bilbo had a very important destiny that only he could fulfill."

I glare at her. "This isn't exactly what I have in mind."

Loraine starts to laugh. "Emma, how often is life *exactly* what we have in mind?"

Silence returns. Loraine is wise enough to let me stew in my own internal conflict. The Meeker property lies just on the outskirts of Santa Barbara. The land is typical of the Gold Coast. It parallels Highway 154 and gives way to vast rolling hills, which descend from the Los Padres National Forest. This is an ideal location for releasing birds of prey due to the miles of open grasslands and valleys that provide swirling wind currents.

I turn right onto a dirt road and shift the Jeep into first gear. The steep hill winds around the hillside like a snake hugging a boulder. After about half a mile, the land begins to flatten out. On the right I see a turnoff with five vehicles, including Parker's Volvo. A small group of people stand talking. Parker is dressed in his tennis whites. I see my student Simon and recognize his younger brother. I park the Jeep next to Parker's car.

Loraine lifts her sunglasses to peer into my eyes. "Which bird do you want to release?" she asks.

A smile consumes my face. Without any hesitation I respond, "The red-tailed hawk."

Loraine pats me on the knee. "She's all yours."

We don't get many female raptors. It is the males who get wounded. The females must be more careful, take fewer risks, and tend to the babies. It is a gift to release any raptor, but a female is a rare treat, and this will be my first.

Raptor releases are carefully distributed to our volunteers as a way of showing appreciation for their contributions. Today, both Loraine and I have the honor of releasing a bird. It has been six months since I had my last release—a falcon.

Loraine and I get out of the Jeep. The day is beautiful. Dramatic white clouds billow over the mountains and are stunning against the sapphire sky. Due to an unusual abundance of winter rain, green grass covers the hillsides and resembles a blanket gently embracing the earth. Spring fills the air and carries the fragrance of new growth. Old oaks dot the cascading hills. In the distance, a large grove of eucalyptus consumes a ravine. Random wildflowers sway to the music of the season.

Parker walks over and gives me a kiss, then lingers, and looks into my eyes as if to evaluate my condition. I reassure him with a smile. He then greets Loraine. Parker lifts the Jeep trunk and takes both crates as I grab the two sets of gloves from the back. Loraine proceeds to greet people and directs them to follow her up the hill. Parker and I fall in behind the group.

129

Simon approaches me with his little brother in tow. I smile at him. "This must be your brother?"

"Yeah, this is Bobby."

I extend my hand to Bobby. "It's nice to meet you."

He gives me a moist and clammy handshake.

"What year are you in high school?" I ask.

"I'll be a sophomore in the fall," he says. The young adolescent slouches in wrinkled clothes. It is difficult for him to maintain eye contact with me.

"I guess I'll be seeing you in a couple of years in my English class," I offer, trying to make conversation. There is something about him that captures my attention: I think it's called *potential.* His wounds radiate from him. Today, perhaps my own wounds make me more sensitive to those of others.

Both boys appear evasive. Clearly, I have touched some nerve.

Bobby kicks a loose stone in the dirt. "I won't be in your class, Mrs. Carter."

"Why is that?"

"I'm not as smart as Simon."

My heart aches for him. His older brother will be going off to a prestigious college and will no doubt be quite successful in whatever he attempts. I'm sure it has been a challenge to follow in Simon's footsteps.

"A lot can happen in two years," I offer.

Bobby looks at me in silence, his face void of any readable emotion.

Loraine has found her release location, a small plateau overlooking a narrow valley. Parker sets down the crates. Loraine addresses the group, "Thank you for coming. Welcome to all of you. My name is Loraine North. I've been working with wounded raptors for thirty years. I run The Raptor Rehabilitation Center. Today we will be releasing two birds." Loraine pauses and gestures to a man with an impressive camera that hangs off his shoulder. "Brandon Locke is here from the *Gold Coast Observer*. He will be taking some photos and doing a story about the rehabilitation center."

Loraine looks at me. "Emma Carter has been volunteering with me for five years, and her contributions are indispensable." I smile at Loraine. Her gaze then turns to Parker. "And this is Parker, Emma's husband. Emma also has some students here from Castio High School." Loraine looks at Simon and gestures that he should introduce himself.

"I'm Simon Kells. This is my younger brother, Bobby." Bobby dips his head with a nod.

Loraine looks to the group but mostly to Brandon Locke. "The Raptor Rehabilitation Center works with about two hundred birds a year. Today we will be releasing a great horned owl and a red-tailed hawk." Loraine puts on her heavy raptor gloves. "It is an accomplishment to rehabilitate a wild animal and successfully return it to its home. This couldn't be done without dedicated volunteers who contribute countless hours of work. This great horned owl was poisoned, probably by eating a mouse or rat that had been poisoned. He has been in rehab for eight months."

I step forward to assist Loraine by tipping the crate back. Loraine bends over and opens the metal door. With some commotion she removes the owl. Once out of the

131

crate, the owl begins to flap his wings and click his beak, eager to be free. Loraine allows the group to get a good look at the owl and appreciate his beauty. Brandon begins to snap photos.

Loraine holds the owl tightly in her extended right hand. "Great horned owls can be as large as twenty-five inches tall and have a wingspan up to five feet. They can weigh up to five pounds. Due to their tremendous strength, they are able to prey upon mammals that exceed their own weight, like skunks or raccoons. They lay one to five eggs each spring, typically in February or March. The eggs take a month to hatch. Because owls are nocturnal, typically we release them at night. Due to the number of barn owls we get in the spring, my aviaries are overflowing. He's ready to go and I need the space, so today is his lucky day!"

Loraine walks toward the edge of the plateau. She positions the owl so that its back is to her chest. She is silent for a moment, then bends her knees and lowers her arms slightly. Loraine gives a jump and springs the bird into the air. The owl catches a wind current and flies away. Our once still and silent audience now claps and cheers for the successful release. Loraine stands with her back to the group and watches the owl. I walk over to her and put my hand on her back. We both stand in silence as we watch the bird fly into the distance and then land in a eucalyptus grove.

I lean close and whisper into Loraine's ear. "I've decided to let Bobby release the hawk."

Loraine turns to look at me, her surprise evident. "Are you sure?"

"Yes, I'm sure."

Loraine nods her head, accepting my decision. Just as we turn around to join the group, Brandon begins to snap photos of Loraine and me. We pose, arms around each other, tightly. In that moment, I am struck by the beauty of our friendship and to the work that brought us together. I am deeply moved by the depth of love that I feel for this woman. I am grateful to participate in work that makes a difference, even if it is on a small level.

Our group chatters enthusiastically. I slip on my new gloves as Loraine steps forward and tips back the remaining crate. Carefully, I open the latched door. The red-tailed hawk wears an ornate leather hood that is secured on one side with a leather string.

After I lift her out of the crate, the hawk flaps her wings defensively. The beauty of this wild creature quiets the group.

I look over at Bobby. "I'm going to have you help me with this bird, Bobby. Are you up for it?"

Bobby appears flabbergasted. "Yes, Mrs. Carter."

Loraine removes her heavy leather gloves and gives them to Bobby. "Here, son, put on these gloves."

I explain to the group, "This female hawk somehow managed to get into oil from the ocean. It's taken five months to get her feathers back to normal."

I stand close to Bobby and can feel his excitement and intimidation. "She weighs about three pounds. You need to be ready to support her body weight when I pass her to you. Put your hand beneath mine. See how my fingers hold the body." Bobby puts his hand under mine. "I'll leave her hood on until you are holding her."

The hawk impatiently flaps her wings. Bobby focuses intently on getting the hawk under control.

"That's good. Keep a strong hold. Let me know when you're ready for me to let go."

Bobby looks at me. "Okay, I guess I'm ready."

"You need to be sure," I say assertively.

"I'm sure."

I remove my hand from supporting the hawk. I untie the hawk's hood and remove it from her head. The bird is amazing—so full of life, so intense, so beautiful. Now, sensing the promise of freedom, the hawk struggles even harder. She attempts to fly while still held captive.

"Bobby, hold on tight; you're doing great."

Bobby is transforming, right there, in front of everyone's eyes. The young man who arrived insecure now seems vibrantly alive. Brandon snaps photos. I step out of the photo frame so that he can pose alone with the hawk. The hawk's wings spread wide, and Bobby smiles, a victorious smile—as if he himself jumped up to the heavens and captured the bird. It is a moment that holds a glimpse of things to come for this young man.

I escort him to the edge of the plateau. "You need to give her a good toss into the air, because she needs to be able to catch the wind current. You will have to bend your knees, just as if you're throwing a basketball, then give a jump, and toss her up."

The group watches in silence.

"Are you ready, Bobby?"

"Yes."

"Okay then, you know what to do," I say as I step away from him.

Bobby follows my directions: bends his knees, jumps, and then tosses the bird into the air. She spreads her wings, gives three strong cries, glides a short distance, and then lands on a bare branch in a nearby oak tree. All of us remain silent. The hawk turns her head and looks at us, as if in acknowledgement. Seconds later she drops off the branch and begins to soar over the open land.

In every raptor release I've witnessed, the birds exhibit a nervous intimation of freedom. Having been earthbound, they must regain their bearings from the sky, the brightness of the sun, and the feel of weightless suspension. To an observer, their intimidation is palpable. It takes the birds a moment to get their bearings—to literally find their wings—and remember what it means to be wild. Every single release is different, and every one rekindles my love of this work and my dedication to rehabilitation.

I pat Bobby on the back. "You did a great job!"

"Thank you, Mrs. Carter!" Bobby nervously glances at his brother. For once he did something Simon has not.

"You're welcome," I say to him, enjoying his enthusiasm. "Bobby, we are always looking for volunteers to help with the birds. If that is something you're interested in, you let me know."

"Yeah, maybe," he hesitates. "Maybe I could do that."

"You know where to find me. Room 1507."

"Okay, I'll think about it," he says.

We return to the group, all of whom fusses over Bobby. Brandon has out his paper and pencil and begins to interview Bobby.

I walk over to Parker. "Thanks for coming, honey," I say with a smile.

"I wouldn't have missed it." His eyes convey love, appreciation, and a dose of pride.

Parker picks up the two empty crates. We say goodbye to the group and walk together to my Jeep.

"That was really nice of you, Emma, to give that boy your release. He'll remember that experience for the rest of his life."

"I hope so."

"I'm sure of it. I think you just inspired a new wildlife biologist."

I start to laugh. "I guess that was the idea."

Parker opens the Jeep trunk and puts in the two empty crates, then closes it. He gives me a quick kiss. "You have yourself a great afternoon. I'll see you a bit later."

"Thank you, honey. Have a good time."

I watch him walk to his car and then pull onto the dirt road. I wave goodbye and blow him a kiss. In response, he smiles and winks. He drives away slowly, trying hard not to leave me in a wake of dust.

Loraine is still saying her goodbyes, but I don't mind waiting. My eyes scan the sky, searching for the hawk. I watch her glide through the air on exhilaration.

The group finally disbands. Loraine joins me beside my Jeep as the caravan of cars leave the hillside. She and I take our place at the end of the line. She looks at me as I turn onto Farmhill Road. "That was a generous gift you gave that young man."

"I think he needed it more than I."

Just up ahead, a massive group of cyclists consumes our lane. There must be a hundred or more, all dressed in neon clothing. They move in synchronized chaos; the spokes in the wheels reflect the sunlight and spin round and round. I take an alternate route.

I sigh and make my confession: "My father was stationed in Korea during the war. A suggestion has been made that he abandoned a woman and child there."

"Well, that is some news," she says. "How did you come by this information?"

"Through a psychic! Roxanne hired a psychic for my birthday. I've never been to one in my life, and now I know why." I hear the disdain in my words.

Loraine takes a moment to think about my revelation before responding. "You seem more concerned about the messenger than the message itself. God works in mysterious ways," she says, staring at me.

I'm shocked. "That's the most sacrilegious thing I've ever heard you say!"

"I'm not here to judge the messengers," she responds. "I'll leave the business of judging to God."

I turn left onto State Street. "To be perfectly honest, I didn't expect that reaction from you."

Loraine reaches over and touches my arm. "Darling, maybe this information has come to you in numerous forms. Maybe you just didn't see or hear it. If this information, regardless of the messenger, heals the wounds of a family, wouldn't that be in accordance with the ways of God?"

I take a deep breath. "Loraine, I don't take this lightly. I'm afraid it's going to *open* wounds, not heal them."

As I turn into Loraine's neighborhood, from out of nowhere a young child rides a tricycle into the street, directly in front of my Jeep. I slam on the brakes. The wheels skid to a stop. Our bodies are instantaneously flung forward, and the smell of rubber fills the car. My heart pounds so loudly that I swear I can hear it reverberating off the windows. We both sit in shock, *stunned* by the near miss. The little girl innocently smiles and waves to us with enthusiasm. The mother, holding the hand of another child, yells at her daughter from the curb and gives us a sheepish acknowledgement, filled with both embarrassment and gratitude.

"Oh my God, I didn't need that!" I say breathlessly. "Sorry, Loraine."

"No, no," she says, "I'm glad you were watching."

With adrenaline still pumping through my veins, I pull into Loraine's driveway. I turn off the engine and face her. "The whole thing overwhelms me. Parker and I don't have children. I let go of that. We let go of that. As a teacher, I love everyone else's children, and that has been enough for me. The fact that my father might have left behind a family makes me sick." I hear my own voice raise a few octaves. "How many more siblings are there?"

"Just take one step at a time," Loraine says to me. She takes off her sunglasses and rubs her eyes as though they have been strained for too long. "Emma, listen to me. I have devoted my life to wounded birds, to heal them and return them to their home in nature. I'm grateful for this work, grateful that it has provided me a mission. But *nothing*, Emma, *nothing*, takes the place of family. If I could find any living family, regardless of how I got the information, I'd do everything in my power to find them."

I sit in silence, allowing her words to permeate my soul and make room for a new perspective.

I look at her face, so filled with love and acceptance. I take her hand and squeeze it in gratitude. "You're right. Thank you, Gandalf."

I open our front door and walk into the house. Before I am able to set down my purse, the phone rings. I lift up the receiver and look at the caller ID to check who is calling.

"Hi, Mom."

"Yeah. I was going to call you; I've just been so busy. How is everything with you?"

Argos comes over to me with his tail wagging. I reach down to pet him, then walk into the living room and sit down.

"Mom, I have something important to talk to you about. Is this a good time for you?" I pause, waiting for her response. "Roxanne threw a little birthday party for me, and there was a woman who..."

I look out our kitchen window. Flowers are in bloom, and peaches are forming on the tree.

I pause, holding the phone, and wait for my mother to finish her sentence. "Yes, I told Sarah all about it. Of course. Yes, I told her what you said about the rings." I watch Parker as he takes his carry-on luggage to the front door. "Mom, Parker is just about to leave, so I need to go. I will. I love you too, Mom. Bye-bye."

I set down the phone and turn to Parker. "My mother sends her regards and wishes you all the best in Boston."

He turns to me. "That's nice. I'm sorry you're not coming with me. I hate to miss your graduation speech."

"I wish I were going with you, too. I could have used my new luggage."

I walk over to Parker and wrap my arms around him. I breathe him in. I always feel nervous when he leaves on trips. I'm acutely aware of his vulnerabilities as a traveler in an unknown city, but mostly I worry about the flight. No doubt, it is a ramification of the times.

"Be safe—and call me," I say, leaning back to look into his eyes.

"You be safe, too. I love you Emma."

"I love you, too."

I walk Parker to the front door. Argos follows. Parker gives Argos a pat on the head. "You take care of Emma for me."

Argos looks at him, and his eyes shift back and forth. At times, I swear that dog understands English.

Parker takes his carry-on luggage and overcoat to the car and puts them in the backseat. He turns and waves to me as he gets into the driver's seat. I wave back and blow him kisses. I shut the front door and walk back to the kitchen.

The newspaper lies abandoned on the countertop. I take the rubber band off of it and flip through the sections. On the front page of the local section, the headline reads:

"WILD BIRDS RELEASED." There is a large colored photo of Bobby holding the hawk. Bobby is smiling and the hawk impressively has its wings fully extended. It is a great photo with the mountains as a backdrop. I lift out the section from the folded paper. Brandon Locke has written an elaborate story. There is a photo of Loraine and me, with our arms around each other, our hearts beaming. I feel my own spirit soar.

Emma Carter
Castio High School Graduation

My mouth goes dry as I wait to be introduced by Dr. Adams, the district superintendent. The high school gymnasium is filled with people who shuffle and move on the bleachers. The audience also consumes hundreds of chairs that are organized on the wood floor. This is the largest audience I have ever spoken in front of. I can't help but wonder why I agreed to this.

Dr. Adams leans into the microphone, "It gives me great honor to introduce Emma Carter. Mrs. Carter teaches English here at Castio High School. She is respected by students, teachers, and staff. Her love of literature is infectious and inspirational. On behalf of all of us, we are delighted for her to give this year's graduation commencement address." A loud applause fills the crowded gymnasium.

I walk to the podium and adjust the microphone. With a quick glance into the audience, I see Ed, Parker's colleague sitting in the second row. His eyes are bright and focused on me. This is so unexpected that I have to regain my center point. I can't imagine why he is here. *Or can I?*

I open my notes. "Thank you very much. I'm honored to give this year's commencement address." I take a moment to breathe. "I often find myself in a mixed bag of emotions at this time of year. After teaching high school English for so many years, you would think I'd be used to the fact that high schoolers actually do graduate and move on with their lives. But each year, I have a bit of postpartum depression when graduation time comes around. In fact, my sister jokes with me that this is why my husband and I don't have children. I would never want to let them leave. Over the years I've come to believe she might be right." I pause to take a sip of water. "Each May I find myself reflecting on the words of Joseph Campbell, a man who spent his entire life devoted to studying world mythologies. He was an esteemed academic at Sarah Lawrence College, where he remained for his entire career. His exploration of *The Hero's Journey* brought him international acclaim. In essence, according to Campbell, the hero must leave home. No foreign lands can be explored, no adventures had, no people met or theories tested, from the comfort of an armchair." I glance over the audience, seeing a few familiar faces. My eyes can't help but to find Ed. His presence is unnerving. I look back to my notes. "Just like the stories, whether it be of Odysseus on his long journey home or Bilbo Baggins fighting a dragon, there will be challenges—it's a given. There will be times when we doubt and question what we're doing—that's a given too. But these challenges are the dragons that we all must meet, compromise with, or slay, because it is only by embracing our challenges that we become the hero in our own story."

A cell phone rings. I look up, momentarily distracted.

Parker Carter
American Psychological Association Conference, Boston

A cell phone rings, blaring into the audience Dudley Do-Right's valiant rescue music. I stop, peer over my reading glasses, and wait for the phone to be turned off.

I use the opportunity to take a sip of water before I begin again. "This historical lineage of the masculine—that has had an endless need to dominate and conquer—comes at a high price to the world. War, destruction, terrorism, technology at our fingertips to do immeasurable damage to the world is not without consequence. Throughout time, the oppression of the feminine has served the masculine."

I pause and look up into the audience. "There is a slow but steady ascension of the feminine. In the last century, women have made their mark on history through voting, the demand for equal pay, the appointment of powerful positions in government and in corporations. Through medical research, women gained the ability to practice birth control, which had an immeasurable social impact of independence. All the while, the masculine has pursued, as James Hillman might say, '*a terrible level of war.*'" I pause to flip a page of my notes.

Emma Carter

I pause to flip a page of my notes. "So my dear graduates, whether it's on to college, trade school, or finding your vocation, may you have a grand adventure!" I briefly look to the graduates, finding the familiar faces that I have grown to love over the last year. "I wish you courage, tenacity, faith and conviction of your own beliefs. I wish you loyal companions and allies. I wish you beauty and a good dose of nature to anchor your feet into the world. Because I believe—without any shred of doubt—that the most extraordinary discovery you will find on your journey will be yourself."

I can feel a lump in my throat growing and my own emotions rising to the surface. I take a sip of water, then turn back to look directly at the graduates. "It has been my deep honor to be one of your high school teachers. Thank you so very much."

Applause fills the auditorium. The high school graduates stand to applaud, and then the audience follows their lead. I take a bow, smile, close my notes, and sit down.

Dr. Adams resumes the graduation proceedings. Each student's name is called and they come forward to receive their degree. Some students are quiet and meek while others dance to express their joy. Random cheers and applause fill the auditorium.

Dr. Adams addresses the graduates with a final congratulation. He has the graduates move their tassels from one side to the other. There is a roar of enthusiasm, and with that, all of the fanfare comes to an end.

Approximately two thousand people stand up and collect their belongings. A crowd of people start to gather around the graduates to congratulate them. Others begin to leave the building like a herd of cattle. The only thing missing is a cloud of dust. The formality of space between strangers is lost to bodies next to each other, often in conversation. In the midst of the exodus, I can't help but wonder how long it will take Ed to make an appearance.

I hear my name called. "Mrs. Carter!"

I turn to see Simon wearing his graduation cap and gown. Next to him is Bobby and who I assume to be their parents. I can't help but notice Bobby's shirt is neatly pressed, a notable difference from the last time I saw him. I make my way toward them.

"Mrs. Carter, your graduation speech was great!" Simon says to me. He turns toward his mother and father. "I'd like to introduce you to my parents."

I shake their hands.

Mrs. Evans smiles at me. "Your graduation speech was memorable. No wonder the students love you so much."

She is a sweet woman. I can see where Simon gets his gentleness. "Thank you, Mrs. Evans."

Mr. Evans looks at me. "We also wanted to thank you for allowing Bobby to do the hawk release. Did you see it in the paper? Brandon Locke wrote a great article."

148

"Yes, he did! The photo of Bobby was nice too." I say, acknowledging Bobby.

Mrs. Evans' pride is evident. "I bought up every newspaper I could get my hands on. It's been mailed to all the relatives!"

"Well, I must admit, it was worth sharing." I turn to Bobby and smile at him.

From the mass of people emerges Ed. He walks up and patiently waits for me to finish with the Evanses.

Mrs. Evans puts her hand on the back of Simon. "We won't keep you. It was very nice to meet you, Mrs. Carter."

I smile at them. "It was nice to meet you as well."

I turn to Simon. "Congratulations, Simon. Keep me posted how you're doing in college."

"Yes, I will," he says to me.

Bobby looks at me and smiles, his eyes actually meeting mine. I feel a small but meaningful shift.

"I'd like to come see you next fall when school starts," he says to me.

"That would be great! I'll look forward to it," I say to him as the Evans family joins the mass of people leaving the lobby of the auditorium.

I turn to Ed. "Hi Ed, what a nice surprise!"

Ed embraces me and lingers, then gives me a kiss on the cheek. I'm surprised by his demonstrativeness.

"Bravo!" he says, his voice filled with enthusiasm. "Parker never told me what a great speaker you are. English would have motivated me more if I'd had a teacher like you." He smiles coyly and begins to laugh loudly and flirtatiously.

149

"Do you know someone who is graduating, Ed?"

"No," he confesses. "I just happened to be in the neighborhood. Parker told me you would give the commencement address. What a shame he missed out on this."

Professional competition has historically existed for Ed toward Parker, and envy has raised its head in odd and unexpected ways. I'm sure Ed is aware Parker is in Boston. I'm surprised Ed isn't in Boston as well. Now he is here at graduation, with no graduate to be a guest of. I'm beginning to wonder if his range of competition expands beyond the academic arena. He assertively takes my elbow and begins to escort me through the crowd. Not wanting to be overly rude, I allow him to do so. He won't get far, and I know this.

I turn to him. "Parker told me you saved the day with Lauren Cooper."

Ed's surprise shows. "He told you? Well, honestly, I'm not sure that I did that much."

"According to Parker, you did," I say to him.

"Perceptions vary so," he replies as we approach the auditorium exit doors. He looks at me seductively. "I do believe a bit of celebration is in order. I would be honored if you would join me for a glass of champagne at the Wine Cellar."

No sooner are his words spoken than I see, standing like the Great Wall of China, my sister Sarah, my brother-in-law, Iain, their two boys, and Savannah and Loraine. They have been waiting at the exit for me. I turn to him. "My family and friends are here, Ed. Let me introduce you." He lets go of my elbow and follows me toward

150

them. I can sense that his fantasy has just been ruined. It is hard for him to hide his disappointment. A quick study, Savannah already has surveyed Ed like he is a fly on a meringue pie.

"Ed, I'd like you to meet my friends and family. This is my sister, Sarah; her husband, Iain, my two nephews, Jason and Evan; and my good friends Savannah and Loraine." Ed is a perfect gentleman and is polished to perfection in social grace. Handshakes are exchanged. Ed pauses with my sister and begins to laugh flirtatiously. "Well, I can see that beauty runs in the family. It is so nice to meet you, Sarah." Sarah smiles at him.

Ed looks at Loraine. "I recognize you from the newspaper article. What noble work you do!" Loraine smiles, suddenly looking flushed. I think it is entirely possible for Ed to charm the pants off a seventy-year-old. He is a wonder to watch.

"Ed is a colleague of Parker's," I offer.

Everyone nods, now understanding the connection.

I turn to Ed. "Thank you for your generous offer. I have to decline. I promised the boys we'd all go out for ice cream."

Upstaged for ice cream! Ed appears to be collecting himself from the blow. I am relieved that I actually had plans and could avoid an awkward situation.

"Well, I'm glad to see you have friends and family to celebrate with," he says gracefully.

"Thank you so much for coming, Ed. It was nice to see you." I smile at him.

He visually acknowledges the lineup, "Nice to meet all of you." He turns and makes his way through the exit

151

doors and out of the building.

Savannah takes me by the arm and whispers, "That man has designs on you, Emma. I can smell it. You better watch yourself." I nod in silent agreement.

I look at my two bored nephews, who have been waiting patiently. "Let's go have ice cream!" With the promise of a sugar fix, both boys are brought back to life.

Parker Carter

"Dr. Carter, Dr. Carter!" I hear my name called as I exit the conference hall in the sea of people.

A middle-aged Korean woman dressed in a conservative navy blue business suit stands waiting at the door. Her formality in both clothing and demeanor is striking. She gently bows to me and then hands me her business card.

"My name is Doctor Chang. I am here from Daegu University in Gyeongsan City, South Korea. I have admired your work for many years. I am honored to meet you." She pauses and smiles at me. "Might I have a moment of your time? I have come all the way from Korea in hopes that I could discuss an opportunity with you."

Naturally, I'm accustomed to meeting people at conferences, but the uncanny coincidence is not lost on me that she is Korean *and actually here from Korea.* I intuitively know that I am the newest recruit to the Ancestors' Conspiracy. I am more generous than I might normally be.

"It's nice to meet you, Dr. Chang. I have a prior commitment that I need to honor, but would be happy to have lunch with you tomorrow."

Dr. Chang's face lights up. "You are a very generous man. This is more than I could have hoped for."

"Why don't we meet right here at 1:00 tomorrow," I say to her.

Clearly pleased, she nods her head. "Yes, I will meet you here, tomorrow, at 1:00." She bows again, and I bow back in response.

We both disappear into the mass of people from different states, different countries and cultures, and different academic backgrounds who all are here to inspire or be inspired, teach and learn, to provoke change and be open to the influence of others, and hopefully find our common threads.

It is clear to me, that whatever I had imagined this international conference would be, it will likely have nothing to do with academics.

Emma Carter

I'm in bed reading. Argos lies beside me on the bed and has made himself right at home. Typically, we don't allow him on the furniture, but when Parker's gone I enjoy the sleeping companionship. I know that Parker will call and he will ask me about graduation. When I think back on the day, my mind wanders to Ed's transparent intensions wrapped in his suave and debonair style. I once saw a children's toy, a stuffed wolf with a sheep's hooded cloak. At the time, it made me burst into laughter. I think that is Ed: a wolf in sheep's clothing. The phone rings. I flip my book upside down on the bed to save my place.

I lift up the receiver to see who is calling: it's an unfamiliar area code accompanied by the words Regency Hotel.

"Hello."

"Hi, honey, it's me."

"You're calling on the hotel phone?"

"Yeah. My cell phone battery went dead. I can't believe I didn't check it. I guess I got distracted with everything. How did your graduation speech go?"

"I feel really good about it, but I'm relieved it's over. It was more stressful than I realized. I met Simon's parents. They were very appreciative of Bobby's hawk release."

"You sound a little odd. Is everything okay?"

My voice sounded fine to me, but I guess there are nuances that can be perceived after so many years together. It is inevitable that I tell Parker about Ed, but frankly I'd prefer not to. I contemplate my ethical options and realize the truth is the inevitable choice. "Well, something strange happened."

"What?"

"I don't want to cause any problems for you." I hesitate. "Ed came to graduation and asked me out for a glass of champagne."

"*What?!*" In my mind I see Parker jumping up from what was once a relaxed position. Indeed I am right, because the next thing I know we are disconnected. I hold the phone, hearing the empty dial tone. I replace the phone in its stand.

I reach over to pet Argos. "Maybe he does have one jealous bone in his body." Argos looks at me and lets out a sigh.

The phone rings.

"Odysseus? Odysseus? Is it you?" I answer the phone with breathless drama.

"Emma, this isn't funny."

In a sex-kitten voice I reply, "Please, call me Penelope. I've been busy unraveling my weaving, hoping you would call." I am amused by my clever application of literature.

"That son of a bitch. Was he trying to pick you up?"

I return to my own voice, knowing that I'm the only one who is entertained. "Well, it's been a long time since I've experienced this kind of thing." I pause and contemplate Ed. "It appeared so."

"What happened?"

"Well, he attended graduation but doesn't know any graduates. That was clue number one. I was surprised he wasn't in Boston with you, but that's beside the point. Then he wanted to take me to the Wine Cellar for champagne to celebrate my successful speech." I selectively leave out the detail of the lingering hug and the escort to the exit.

"I can't believe the nerve of him. Who does he think he is? I'm furious. Absolutely furious."

"Honey, don't get so riled up. It's not worth it. You handled Lauren, and I handled Ed. Actually, I think those two deserve each other."

Parker is silent.

"Honey?"

"Yeah, I'm here."

"Take a couple of deep breaths and let this go. Honestly, it's not worth getting upset over."

"Easier said than done."

"Maybe I shouldn't have told you," I offer.

"Of course you needed to tell me. I'll calm down."

"Let's talk about you. How did your speech go?" I ask, trying to change the subject.

"It went well. I just can't believe Ed. What an opportunist!"

"Let's not allow our conversation to be ruined. I've been looking forward to your call. How was the rest of your day?"

I hear Parker take a deep breath. "I met a woman today, Dr. Chang. She is here from South Korea. She said she came to the conference in hopes of discussing an

157

opportunity with me." Parker pauses momentarily. "Looks like I'm the newest recruit in the Ancestors' Conspiracy."

Now I'm the one sitting straight up in bed. "You've got to be kidding! *What* opportunity?"

"I'll find out tomorrow," he says to me. "We're going to have lunch."

"Oh, my god. This is unbelievable! What else did she say?"

"Not much. I didn't give her a chance. I needed to meet Darwin Miller."

"You're having lunch with her tomorrow?!"

"Yes."

"Will you call me after lunch?"

"I could, but honestly, I'd rather wait till tomorrow night. I've got a really busy day tomorrow, and I'm having dinner with a few people from APA."

I attempt to cover my disappointment. "Okay, I'll be patient."

"Are the girls still coming over for dinner tomorrow?"

"Yeah, we should be done by 9:00."

"I'll call you around 9:30."

"That'll be great." I feel myself lost in thought. "This Korean story seems to have a life of its own and evidently will move forward with or without me."

"Tomorrow should be an interesting day. How is Argos?"

I look at Argos, who is peacefully asleep. "He's fine. His quality of life has been elevated. He is sleeping with me. He's a horrible bed hog. He snores *and farts*." I can't help but smile. "At least you don't snore," I offer as I burst into laughter.

I can imagine Parker smiling at the other end of the phone. "We can both be grateful for that," he says to me.

There is a momentary silence.

"So Emma," his voice shifts into deep coaxing. "What weaving project are you unraveling?"

Without missing a beat, my seductress returns, "My panties—I've been unraveling my panties."

I reach over and turn off the light, nestle down under the covers, and make myself comfortable. My book now closes as the blankets shift. I willingly lose my place. I listen to Parker's words and voice as he seduces me into submission.

The moonlight comes through the window and lights softly on my face. My eyes close, and my body drifts into sleep.

> I am in Nordstrom's shoe department shopping with Savannah. I am trying to find a pair of shoes. I turn to Savannah. "I'd like a pair of practical shoes, something comfortable." I pick up a tan Mephisto shoe. Savannah looks bored by my choice. A salesman, as handsome as Prince Charming, notices me holding the shoe and walks over to us.
>
> "May I help you?" he asks with a dazzling smile.
>
> "I'd like to try these in a size eight," I say to him. My heart skips a beat.

"You can't go wrong with these shoes. They'll be a good investment for you."

I hand the salesman the Mephisto shoe and he leaves, taking it with him. Savannah and I sit down on the couch, waiting for the salesman to return. Savannah turns to me and says, "I just love this place. It's where dreams come true."

Prince Charming returns, balancing seven different boxes of shoes. He looks at me with deep regret. "I'm sorry. We don't have that shoe in your size. I brought you some other comparable shoes to try."

I feel a sense of loss. I turn to Savannah. Although we do not speak, she clearly feels my disappointment.

The prince, eager to make amends, carefully takes a shoebox as though it's sacred and lifts the lid. He unfolds the tissue and holds up a shoe, as if presenting a thing of wonder and beauty. There, gleaming in the light, is a red sequined shoe. They are in fact, Dorothy's ruby slippers, from The Wizard of Oz. With award-winning salesmanship, he smiles at me. "This is an excellent walking shoe with great support. They are perfect for traveling."

I feel myself hesitate. "They aren't exactly what I had in mind."

"Very well. Let me show you this next pair," he says as he lifts the next shoebox lid.

He unfolds the tissue and holds up the shoes. Again, they are ruby slippers. He introduces them as though they are an entirely new pair of shoes. "This has been an excellent seller. The color is so versatile—they go with anything! They are perfect for day or evening wear."

Again, I decline the shoes.

This parade continues one pair at a time. Each shoe is introduced, held up, and admired. Each shoe is treated as though it is entirely different, when they are all exactly the same. Surrounding the couch, where Savannah and I sit, are scattered shoeboxes, each holding ruby slippers. Savannah silently watches. The salesman puts the sixth pair of ruby slippers on my feet. I stand and walk around. I return and smile at him, beginning to feel embarrassed. "No, I'm sorry. These feel a bit too tight."

Throughout all of this, the handsome shoe salesman has remained completely enthusiastic and assured of himself and the mission.

He looks at me. "This last shoe is entirely different from what you asked for, but my heart tells me it's right for you. They have character!"

He lifts the shoebox lid to reveal another pair of ruby slippers. I take the shoes from the box and put them on my feet. I stand, pivot my

161

toes, and admire the beauty and brilliance of the shoes.

Savannah sits up in the couch and her voice fills with wonder. "Emma, they do have character!"

I turn to the salesman, "You're absolutely right; these are just perfect!"

I leave the shoes on and hand him my American Express card. It catches the light and gleams across the store. Over the intercom I hear a deep man's voice say: "American Express. Anywhere in the world you go—we go."

I wake up alone in the bed. Argos has left. The dream is vivid in my mind. I think of the ruby slippers and their role in Dorothy's journey. I realize in the dream that I had to accept the shoes—put them on myself. No man can place destiny upon my feet. To embrace fate is my decision—and my decision alone. I feel an internal shift in my heart, as though a sense of peace was infused in my moonlit dream. I get up, go to the bathroom, turn on the faucet, and let the water run.

Water streams out of the kitchen faucet, and I fill the kettle. I look out the window to the backyard, appreciating the beauty of the flowers. Having eaten, Argos peacefully lies on the floor watching me.

I walk into the living room to put on a CD. I find a very specific song, "Sigma" from Secret Garden. It is a prayer sung with a palpable holiness that is appropriate for this moment: I walk toward the China cabinet. My hand slowly turns the key to unlock the lock. I open the glass door and remove the Asian cup and saucer. I take it back to the kitchen and carefully wash and dry it.

Intuitively, I know who the Korean woman is in the cup. I know the hanbok, the hair perfectly combed into a tight bun, the shape of her face, the curve of her lips, and the eyes that stare back and challenge me. If she could speak from the porcelain, I know that she would suggest that I eat fish to be more flexible.

I hold the teacup up to the light to look at the image of the woman at the bottom of the cup. In-sook stares back at me. My hands begin to shake. I put the cup back on the saucer and take it to the dining room, setting it on the table. I return to the kitchen and finish making tea. I pour milk into an ornate pitcher and give the tea a final stir. I carry the teapot and pitcher of milk into the dining room.

I sit down in front of the teacup and fold my hands in prayer. Tears begin to stream down my cheeks as I pray to God and whoever else will listen. I pray that I have strength and courage. I pray that I can do what my father could not. I pray for wisdom, guidance, and acceptance. I take the teacup—in both hands—lift it to my lips and drink. In a ritualistic way, I silently accept my fate.

Savannah Jones

"Emma, it's me, Savannah," I yell as I open Emma's front door.

Argos comes barrelin' round the corner. I'm not too crazy 'bout dogs, but Argos has found a way into my heart—and evidently—me into his. I bend over and greet him, "Hey Argos, how are ya?"

He begins a throaty growl, and shoves his nose up into the air, as if tryin' to answer me.

"Come on in," I hear Emma call.

I go into the kitchen, a bottle of wine in one hand, my purse in the other. I set the wine on the counter and hook my purse over the bar stool.

Emma stands beside a pile of roses. She's wearin' decorative leather gardenin' gloves and a cookin' apron. The roses are a sight: red, yellow, white, pink, and deep raspberry blossoms.

I seize the moment. "We haven't had much of a chance to see each other lately. I didn't want to bring this up at the graduation, and I didn't want to talk about it on the phone. I thought you might be mad at me, after the grocery store, and you squeezin' them peaches and all."

"Well, I was a bit miffed in the moment. But I also know there's some truth to what you said."

"Truth in which part? The peaches or the psychic?"

"Both."

"Does this mean I'm forgiven?"

Emma smiles at me. "Totally."

"Thank God! I can't stand the thought of you bein' mad at me!"

We give each other a quick hug to seal the deal. My attention turns back to the roses. I look at Emma. "I bet you know the name of every rose you have."

Emma smiles at me as she takes off her gloves. "I do," she says, and begins to point to them like she is introducin' me to friends. "New Day," she says to a yellow rose that is so bright it makes my teeth ache. "I love New Day, but it's a weak shrub," Emma says quietly, so the blossom won't hear. "I have trouble getting it to bloom," she confesses.

Emma pauses momentarily, "Chrysler Imperial," she says as she points to the next rose. "It's a true classic for those who love red roses. It's a hearty shrub, always dependable for producing abundant roses." She lifts a raspberry rose out of the pile and hands it to me. Her voice gets all soft and misty, "This one is Yves Piaget."

I take it from her, put it under my nose and am instantly swoonin' like a schoolgirl in love. "It's a French rose," Emma says, raisin' her eyebrows. "I purchased it from that rose nursery in Carpinteria. You know that place right? Acres of roses growing on the hillside like a vineyard." She doesn't wait for me to respond and instead proceeds with the introductions. "The Peace rose is a must for every rose garden," she says pointing to a rose blushed with the kiss of dawn.

If I were a rose in Emma's garden, I wonder how I would be introduced: "A bold perfume, uniquely original with a full blossom and ample thorns."

"Which rose are you?" I ask her.

I do believe she has contemplated the question. She picks up a soft pink rose that resembles a peony. "Kathryn Morley," she says as she tilts the blossom for me to smell. The fragrance is that of a dream, softly perfumed but not overpowerin'. She takes a whiff herself and then sets it back onto the pile. No further words are needed.

"Savannah, how about if you arrange the roses for me?" She hands me the rose clippers. "The blossoms will last longer if you cut them under running water."

"Whatever you say, Martha." I take the cutters from her hands, turn on the faucet and begin to cut the rose stems one at a time and put them into the crystal vase.

Emma's kitchen reflects hours of work. There is a prepped salad, green beans waiting to be put into boilin' water, and a smell from the oven that is so divine it would make any guest thrilled to have a place at the table. Ever hopeful, Argos watches our every move.

The doorbell rings. Emma and Argos go to the front door. Sarah and Roxanne have arrived at the same time. There is a boisterous exchange of greetin'. I can hear them clearly. All the women gravitate to the kitchen. I set down the rose clippers, turn off the water, and give Sarah and Roxanne a kiss. Roxanne has a bouquet of blue and white irises that she gives to Emma. With polished grace, Emma accepts the flowers and plants a kiss on Roxanne's cheek. She then finds a vase and puts the bouquet in water, sets the flowers down, and goes to the fridge, taking out a chilled bottle of wine.

"What can I do to help?" asks Roxanne.

Emma hands the bottle of Rombauer Chardonnay to Roxanne with a corkscrew. "Will you do the honors?" asks Emma.

"Rombauer! My favorite," Roxanne says with a smile.

"I thought that would make you happy," says Emma.

Roxanne takes the corkscrew and opens the wine like she is a pro. The cork gives a solid "pop." Roxanne takes the opened bottle and goes to the dining room.

Emma unscrews the top off a bottle of Perrier. "Sarah, would you please pour this water for the table?

"Sure," says Sarah, as she takes the bottle and goes to the dining room.

Emma's focus shifts to the salads. She and I are once again in the kitchen alone. She says to me, "I had the funniest dream last night, and you were in it."

"What was it about?"

"We were together at Nordstrom's and I was shopping for shoes. The salesman was a gorgeous hunk of a man! He was such a gentleman." Emma says to me, still swoonin'.

"Girl, that is a wild dream. Let's see . . . Prince Charmin' puttin' shoes on your feet. There's no big mystery here!"

Emma starts to laugh. "You're so funny!" she says. "Actually, that same thought crossed my mind. He was wonderfully charming, and I have to tell you, he looked *mighty fine,* Savannah."

I look at her. "What'ja buy?"

"I was looking for some practical shoes," she says.

Emma is as transparent as cellophane around a bowl of fruit. "Emma, honey, I didn't ask what you were looking for. *I asked what you bought.*"

Emma looks at me, slightly embarrassed. Caught in a web of her own omission, she leans in and whispers, "I bought Dorothy's ruby slippers." Her cheeks turn a rosy pink, just like the Kathryn Morley rose. A smile consumes my entire face.

Emma turns back to her tasks and puts the green beans into boiling water. She removes beautifully browned stuffed chicken breasts from the oven. Roxanne and Sarah walk back into the kitchen but are busy talking to each other.

"Emma, did Prince Charmin' put those shoes on your feet?" I ask her.

"Well . . . funny you should ask. No, I put them on myself," she says as she arranges each piece of baked chicken on a plate with some couscous.

"I think your life is about to get *real interestin'*," I say to her. Emma looks at me without expression. She knows what I mean.

I have saved the yellow roses—the ones that hurt my teeth—for last. I carefully select where to put them. I find some irony in their name: New Day. I take the bouquet and put it on the dining room table.

Meanwhile, Emma drains the beans and proceeds to put them on the plates. The focus has now shifted to dinner, and there is a collective appreciation of the main course. Emma takes warm bread out of the oven and puts it in a basket. Each woman takes her plate and goes to the dining room.

The bouquet of roses graces the table as everyone takes a seat. Glasses are raised for a toast. "Here's to us," I say, "and to Emma for cookin'." Glasses clink, and everyone is dressed in happiness.

I turn to Roxanne. "What is happenin' with your job? Are you taking the promotion?"

"I've decided not to," she says. "It's a huge relief. I know it's the right decision. I would have to compromise myself too much."

Sarah is stunned. "I'm surprised! I was sure you would accept that offer. What made you change your mind?"

Roxanne hesitates and chooses her words carefully, "Well, to be perfectly honest, that reading from Amber. Although she didn't really tell me anything I didn't already know, she framed the information differently. It somehow gave me clarity."

Sarah gets all bright-eyed. "Speaking of Amber, I'm still regretting I was unable to come to the birthday party. Emma told me all about it."

There is silence waitin' for Emma's reaction. This is the first time we have all been together since that fateful night. Of course, we are all dyin' to know the update. Roxanne and I have had several conversations behind Emma's back, but no one wants to ask. I, personally, have decided to forget about the Korean. For the sake of our friendship, better to let some things go.

Roxanne takes a sip of wine and then sets down her glass. "Well, that birthday party was a little different than I expected," she confesses.

Sarah looks at Emma. "Have you told them about what has happened since the party?"

"No, I haven't," replies Emma. "This is the first time we've been together."

"Well, aren't you going to tell them?" Sarah asks impatiently. She has good intentions, but I can tell Emma isn't quite ready to be pushed into the deep end of the pool.

Emma awkwardly glances at me. "It looks like what Amber said could be true." She pauses, letting the information take hold. "I talked to our mother. She said our father gave her a gold ring that had been his. They had it resized, and she wore it for years. Later, after they were divorced, she sold it at a pawnshop. The man told her it was a Korean wedding ring. For some time, our dad sent money every month to Korea for a little boy to attend school. Supposedly, the boy was the child of a family he met there."

"Does your mother believe that was his child?" asks Roxanne.

"She believes it's possible," Emma says, looking at Roxanne.

"What are you going to do now?" I say to Emma.

Emma pauses and looks at her sister. "I'm not sure. Sarah and I haven't gotten that far."

"I think this is *your* project, Emma!" Sarah says, her face all pinched tight.

Emma is stunned by her abrasiveness. "Why is it all my responsibility?" she says defensively.

Sarah looks at her. "This information didn't come knocking on my door. You know why? I'm not home."

171

Roxanne and I shoot each other a look. It's a contemporary showdown at the O.K. Corral. It's hard to know if there will be causalities.

Sarah takes aim: "I'm driving Jason to basketball. Evan needs to go to the tutor. We have one dog, two cats, a gerbil, and four guinea pigs. Iain often has to work on the weekends. For god's sake, aside from all the family responsibilities, I'm running a small petting zoo." Sarah pauses but only to catch her breath and reload. "Emma, no offense, but you have an independent husband and an old dog. Let's face it; you're a better bet than me. I'll be your cheerleader from the sidelines." With her chamber empty, Sarah holsters her gun and it hangs smokin' at her side.

There is a long silence. Emma is offended. I know that look and try my best to tend to the wound. "My, oh my, but you are a wonderful cook, Emma! This dinner would make my grandmother proud!" I offer Emma a conciliatory wink and a smile.

Roxanne ignores the lingering smoke. "This is all about timing. Why now? Why did this information come forward after all these years? That's what I find fascinating." She pauses. "I have to agree with Sarah. The information chose you. As fate would have it, Sarah wasn't even at the party."

Roxanne takes a sip of wine. No one dares to say a word. Roxanne looks at Emma. "In Amber's book . . ."

"Amber's book! *Amber has a book?*" Emma says incredulously.

Roxanne's mouth is still open, words waiting to be said. "Yes, it's called *Listening to the Oracle*. That's how I met her. I went to her book reading and signing at Chelsie's."

172

Emma starts to laugh. "You've got to be kidding."

"No. How did you think I found her?" asks Roxanne.

This is too much for me to resist. Emma glares at me, but I can't stop myself. "The Yellow Pages–under Party Entertainment!" I offer, with dramatic flair and a smile.

Roxanne looks at Emma. "You don't find a woman like that in the Yellow Pages."

"So I'm told," replies Emma, now sensin' there is more than one loaded gun in the room.

Roxanne leans into Emma. "Amber is Dr. Amber Nelson. She has a PhD in anthropology. Her specialization is divination. She lives here in the winter and in England in the summer. I managed to persuade her to come to your birthday party. She is a famous writer and lecturer."

Now that Amber's credentials have been established, Emma has been put in her place. She sits quietly. I can just see her wheels turnin'.

"So anyway," says Roxanne, "Amber talks about synchronicities in her book. These meaningful events provide a road map from the divine. Our lives—this culture—has become so busy, so intense, we don't recognize divine intervention, even when it happens. In addition, we are getting farther and farther removed from nature, from life in nature. Historically, cultures looked to the land formations, trees, birds, weather, and clouds for messages. Now we live in concrete jungles, drive our cars talking on cell phones, and eat foods filled with chemicals."

"I believe that synchronicities are messages. I also believe that dreams can be profoundly informative," I say, lookin' at Emma, to make my point.

173

"What does Parker have to say about all this?" asks Sarah.

"Coincidentally, he had lunch today with a woman who flew to Boston from South Korea in hopes to meet with him."

"There you have it," says Roxanne. "Synchronicities at work!"

"You didn't tell me this!" says Sarah.

"Parker just told me about it last night. I'll let you know what happens." I can tell Emma is itchin' to change the subject. She looks at me. "So what about you—what's happening?"

Roxanne interrupts. "Before we change the subject off this whole Korea thing, did you guys have a chance to go to that Korean restaurant that was on Stanton Street? It was amazing! I'm so disappointed that it closed."

Emma is caught off guard, her filter down. Her voice raises two octaves higher. "What do you mean it's closed?" Emma's jaw literally drops. I reach over with my index finger to gently lift the bottom of her chin.

She turns to me smilin'. "Thank you for that assistance, Savannah," her filter now securely in place.

"Well, evidently the owner and the chef moved here from South Korea and there was some family responsibility that required them to return to Korea. They were only open for two months. I'm so bummed. It was really an exceptional restaurant."

I look at Emma. "Do you have somethin' to share? Have you been eatin' Korean food?" I ask, my teeth all bright from my recent dental cleanin'.

"My god, Savannah, you don't miss a beat!"

"Well why should I? I find you very entertainin'." I look at her and wink.

"Parker and I went there once. And I do have to agree with you, Roxanne, it really was exceptional. It was a memorable dinner. It's definitely a loss to the community. Parker's going to be disappointed." Emma takes a sip of wine.

Sarah gives a long sigh as if she is slightly bored. "Okay, I really am ready to talk about something else. Savannah, what about you?"

It is hard for me to hide my excitement, so I decide not to. "The gallery in San Francisco wants to do a private openin' of my work as a fund-raiser for Children and the Creative Arts. It's an after-school program."

Emma lifts up her wine glass. "Here's to you!" Glasses clink together. "Savannah, that's great! I'm really proud of you," says Emma.

"We'll all be able to say we knew you when . . ." says Sarah, laughing.

"Is Brian going with you to San Francisco?" asks Roxanne.

"Yeah, and I'm ecstatic! What would my family in South Carolina say now? This is more than I ever had imagined, and I've got a good man on my arm. Life is just fine. Just fine."

"When is the show?" asks Sarah.

"In August. I've got plenty to do between now and then," I reply.

Roxanne looks at me and then Sarah. "I think there is a trip to San Francisco in our future."

175

"I do believe there is," says Emma, as she smiles at me.

"We should solidify a date. My calendar starts to get really full," adds Sarah.

"There is nothin' I would love more that to have my dear friends at my show in San Francisco. On some days, life just feels too good to be true."

Roxanne looks at Emma. "That was a great dinner. Thank you," she says.

We all chime in our appreciations as we get up from the table, taking our dishes with us. In the kitchen, Roxanne rinses the dishes and loads them into the dishwasher. Laughter and conversation continues. Emma wraps up the leftovers and puts them in the fridge. I wipe off the table. Argos lends his support with hopeful anticipation of food.

"Just leave the wine glasses. I need to do those by hand," says Emma.

Emma puts a drain stopper in the sink. She puts down a rubber sink liner and then squirts dishwashing soap in the sink as the hot water pours in. Bubbles fill the kitchen sink. Emma's hands swish them around.

Emma Carter

Bubbles overflow the bathtub. My hands swish them around. The warm water feels divine as I relax and lean back against the tub. Argos lies on the mat in the bathroom watching me, as his eyes struggle to remain focused. Next to him sits the phone. Candles around the tub cast a warm glow into the room. I close my eyes. It is a peaceful moment.

The phone interrupts my silence. Argos sits up, now alert and watching me. I quickly dry my hand on a towel, pick up the phone, and look at the caller. It's Parker. "Hello?"

"Hi honey, how are you?" Parker says.

"I'm great! How was your day?" I ask, sitting up in the tub.

"Eventful."

"I've been dying to know."

There is a momentary pause on the other end of the phone. "Well, it looks like we're going to South Korea. I had lunch with Dr. Chang. Next July there will be a big international conference in Seoul. She is organizing the speakers and wants me to present. I'm a surprising choice for a culture that remains male dominated, but she clearly understands this."

I'm stunned. The words seem to have lost themselves between my mind and my mouth.

"Emma, are you there?" asks Parker.

"Yes, I just don't know what to say."

"I thought it was best to just be honest with Dr. Chang. I told her that your father might have left behind a child from the Korean War. Our trip would be two-fold: I will fulfill my obligations of the conference, but we will also pursue finding family while in Korea."

I feel my emotions well up within me. "Oh my god."

"There's more. Dr. Chang said this isn't uncommon. Korea is supportive and organized in efforts to connect families. Dr. Chang's sister works in social services in Seoul. Although this isn't her professional area, her sister may be able to assist in the process. This will give you a year to research. I have her sister's e-mail address. Dr. Chang recommended you find the photo and send it via e-mail attachment to her sister. She also recommended you send some photos of your dad from that time period."

I try to collect myself. "Are you there?" asks Parker.

"Yes. It is just a bit overwhelming, that's all. What are the chances that this would happen?"

"It seems obvious the issue isn't going away."

"Yes, you're right. I don't think it is going away. I think I just need a little time to catch up with reality."

"Well, you have a year to get used to the idea. That should help. How was your dinner?"

"Really fun, but my sister was a bit of a pill. She doesn't want to help with the Korean situation. She is supportive of me doing it, but she doesn't have the time to help."

"Are you surprised?" asks Parker.

"Well, no, not really. It's just the way she phrased it that was offensive."

"You know Sarah."

"Yeah, I know Sarah." I pause. "I'll look for the photo tomorrow."

"Good luck with that." I can hear the empathy in his voice.

"Can I tell you one more thing? It's not urgent, but it's just kind of . . . odd."

"Sure, what is it?" asks Parker.

"Well, last night at dinner, Roxanne brought up that Korean restaurant that we went to. Evidently it was only open for two months. The owner and chef needed to return to Korea due to a family obligation. It just seems kind of strange."

There is silence at the other end of the phone and I can tell that Parker is contemplating his response. "That is curious." He treads gingerly. "But I can imagine this kind of thing happens on a regular basis. People move somewhere and then have to return home due to extenuating circumstances."

"Yeah, I think you're right. How was your dinner with the APA people?" I ask, changing the subject.

"Productive. It's always helpful to have inside information about pending changes," says Parker.

There is a moment of silence over the phone. I'm distracted by thoughts of going to Korea to find my brother.

Parker pulls me back. "I'm looking forward to coming home tomorrow. I should be in around 9:00 tomorrow night."

179

"Okay, well, you have a good flight. I love you."

"I love you, too."

I set down the phone and lean back in the tub, slipping down into the warm water. I am eye level to the bubbles. There are bubble mountains, valleys, and rivers where the bathtub water is revealed. I sit up, collect the bubbles, and with care and accuracy I sculpt Mount Fuji down toward my feet. I know that Mount Fuji is in Japan, but it is an iconic Asian mountain and the most familiar to me. My Mount Fuji stands tall and majestic; each tiny bubble contains an iridescent dream. I lean back, proud of my ingenuity, and imagine the beauty of the Far East and its exotic lands.

Emma Carter

A heat wave has hit the central coast. Temperatures soar into the low nineties. This unseasonable weather—for early June—has sent people swarming to the beaches and has northbound traffic backed up for miles.

I, on the other hand, will not be lounging on the sand under an umbrella with a novel in my hand. Today, I have accepted the daunting task of finding old photos, one in particular. I summon my inner warrior to face the utter clutter and chaos of our garage.

We moved into this house two years ago and simultaneously took on a major renovation. Between working full time and having laborers in the house, our garage took the brunt of it. Although it is a two-car garage, we've never been able to park in it. After the remodel was done, we simply ran out of energy. Both Parker and I keep a tidy house, but there's something about the garage that overwhelms us. If anyone should see it—which I avoid—I find myself embarrassed and immediately explain all of the reasons why we've never cleaned it.

I stand outside, wearing flip-flops, shorts, and a T-shirt, no bra, and hold a tall plastic tumbler of ice water. My faithful companion, Argos, stands next to me. I brace myself for the project. Part of me had hoped that some fairy or group of elves miraculously took pity on us and addressed what we have not. No such luck. Argos looks into the garage and begins to whimper.

"You're not kidding," I say to him.

The clutter and disarray of the garage is shocking. Boxes are piled high; stacks of wood from the remodel are pushed against the wall. All kinds of building supplies and tools appear abandoned. There is extra furniture: an armoire, a chest of drawers, and extra chairs for our dining room table. Bicycles hang suspended from the rafters, and downhill skis rest against the shelves. Our Christmas tree is carefully balanced on its side in the rafters; it is obvious we shop at Costco. There is a lifetime supply of toilet paper, paper towels, and laundry detergent. A fifty-pound bag of dog food and a fifty-pound bag of birdseed rest against the cupboards. It is easy to feel defeated at the mere sight of it all.

Argos intuitively knows this will take a while. He lets out a deep sigh and lays down to sleep in the sun.

I find a small open space to set down my tumbler of ice water. I begin to wade through the disaster area and make my way to the back of the garage so that I can open the door for cross ventilation.

I haven't even started, and sweat is already dripping off my face. I look at the cabinets mounted on the wall. They are filled with old books and a few stray knickknacks. Boxes are piled on top of each other on an old metal shelf. I see evidence of mice. So I will not only be dealing with dirty boxes but mouse shit as well. *Great.* My mood is improving by the minute.

182

I begin by throwing empty boxes onto the driveway. I see that Argos has relocated himself beneath the shade of a tree. Startled, he raises his head to look at me. Convinced there is no real threat, he lays back down onto the warm cement. The Samsung television box goes flying through the air, quickly followed by the Uniden box that once held five thousand sheets of paper. While tossing the weed-whacker box, I trip over the birdseed and nearly do a face plant. *What the hell!"*

Parker always wants to save boxes in case something is wrong with the purchase. But now I'm facing all of this consumerism, and it makes me feel slightly nauseated. *How have we accumulated all of this stuff?*

I can feel myself becoming irritated at Parker. *Why isn't he here to help?* How about my sister, Sarah? Couldn't she be here helping? I also feel a welling anger toward my father. I'm ready to be mad at everyone. How did I get elected for this job? I know what this garage looks like. I know why we've avoided dealing with it. What made me think I could actually find *one photo in all of this . . .*

this . . .

shit!

It was ridiculous for me to believe it was possible.

Sweat drips down my face. I take the front of my T-shirt to towel off the moisture. I look at the stacked boxes. At least I had the foresight to mark the contents of the various boxes: craft supplies, Christmas ornaments, miscellaneous fabric, Parker's college memorabilia, my high school stuff, and there, toward the back, is a box titled "Old Photos." I feel my heart rise, as if some form of victory has taken hold. I grab the box and pull off the packing tape. There are old photos. There are pictures of Parker and I when we were first together, some random travel photos, pictures of our parents, and pictures of Argos as a puppy. I feel myself going down memory lane, and it is a welcomed reprieve. These are sacred memories, and despite the way they are stored, I treasure them. I take the box and set it outside of the garage. I think this is a worthy organizational project for next winter.

I turn back and look at the garage. Defeat takes hold and I call out loud, *"Okay Dad, you need to help me! Where is the photo? If you want me to do this, I need you to help me. I cannot do it on my own."* I can hear an emotional element to my own voice.

I step back into the garage to take a drink of water. As I raise the glass, there, smack-dab in the middle of the water is a bee doing the breaststroke. I search for stray piece of sandpaper and scoop him out. He flies away and I set down the water. I am on the verge of crying. This is simply too much. There are a million other things I would rather be doing. This is a Bilbo Baggins moment and not exactly what I had in mind for today *or maybe ever.*

In-sook

"Dad, I can't do this alone," Emma calls out. I hear her desperation. I stand in the garage wearing my blue hanbok, my hair neatly pulled back into a tight bun. I look around the garage at all the mess. For those of us from rural South Korea, this is inconceivable. *Inconceivable.*

"Do you really believe your father will come to help you? I spent a lifetime calling to him, praying, begging to the gods. You know nothing of this." I pause and glance around. "You are like your father. He had so much and always wanted more."

Argos is now sitting up and barking at me. He sees what Emma cannot.

Sweat is profusely dripping off Emma's face. I sit down in a plastic-covered chair and cross my legs to watch the show. She moves a stack of boxes, rearranging them: *getting warmer.*

"Dad! You need to help me. *This is about you; this is not about me!*" Emma yells. Tears are not far away.

I take pity on her, but as much as I would like to help her, I cannot. This is her initiation and she must fight for it; otherwise she will not have the determination and strength she needs. She alone must be worthy of the prize."

185

Emma shifts some boxes around on the shelf. She sees a small box labeled "Special/Miscellaneous." She pulls it forward and tears the tape off the top. In the box are beautiful rice bowls with an image of flowers, a framed award, and other random trinkets. Emma takes out the rice bowls and sets them to one side. In the box is a manila envelope. She opens it and takes out the contents. There are old photos of her dad and the *one* photo she has been looking for of me.

Emma's breath escapes her. "I found it," she whispers.

I watch her face change, like the intricate components of a watch, each piece turning, precisely fitting into place. It's all coming together for her: the teacup, the waitress at the restaurant, and the woman from her dream. She turns the photo over. It reads: In-sook 1952.

"Oh my God. I can't believe it," she whispers.

Emma takes the photo, walks toward me, and perches on a large toolbox. She looks at the photo and touches it with her index finger, as if trying to reach back through time. "You look so happy and beautiful," Emma says to the photo. "I'm so sorry if my father wronged you. *From the depths of my heart, I am so deeply, deeply sorry.*" Tears run down Emma's face.

"I am sorry too," I say to her, knowing that she cannot hear me.

I take her in, all of her genuine kindness, her pure and authentic goodness. It is the empathy I have longed for over my lifetime. Emma is a balm for my soul, and I feel the weight on my heart being liberated. I wipe my own tears away. She and I, in this unlikely place, are now linked through time. She is a worthy advocate, and I am deeply grateful to Randall for having such a daughter.

Emma Carter

"Argos! Why are you barking? It's okay. I'm done now."

Argos is fully animated and looking into the garage, his nose waving in the air as if desperately trying to understand something.

I put the box back in its place and insert the photo of In-sook back into the manila envelope. I cradle the rice bowls in my arm.

"I found what I needed, Argos."

I step out, into the bright sun, my eyes squinting from the light. It is a new day. With my free hand I push the remote to close the garage door. Together, Argos and I walk side by side back to the house.

Emma Carter

I am sitting in front of my computer drinking from the Asian cup that my sister gave me. The photo of In-sook is now beautifully framed and sits on my desk. Through time, she smiles at me and is a reflection of acceptance and love. Two books about Korea are off to one side. Through the window, I see a view of the backyard. The afternoon light shines onto my desk. With fall approaching, the peach tree has turned yellow. I take a sip of tea and push "send" on my e-mail.

Emma Carter

Dawn has begun to brighten the sky with a golden hue. The peach tree is barren, reflecting winter slumber. I take another sip of tea. I'm still in my pajamas and wrapped in the warmth of my robe. There's part of me that would still like to be in bed next to Parker, but my curiosity won out. There are now four books about Korea on my desk. My computer reads: "You have two unread messages." The screen opens to reveal a string of past messages from Korea.

Emma Carter

I sit at my desk and take another sip of tea. It is dusk. The warmth of the setting sun reflects on my office walls. The small pink blossoms of the peach tree hold the promise of new growth and beginnings.

Emma Carter

♦

I raise my teacup to my lips and drink. I am sitting at my desk, surrounded by books about Korea. Summer is in full blossom, and through the window, I see small peaches forming on the tree. I have carefully selected my travel clothes, preparing for the long journey to Korea.

I search through my e-mails, just in case there is one final message before our trip. Parker walks into my office. "Emma, we need to leave. Are you ready?" He walks over to me and takes a sip of tea from my cup—*the cup*.

"Yes, I am ready, but I thought I should check one more time to see if there are any messages from Du-na. How are we ever going to thank this woman? No gift could ever equal what she has accomplished."

"We really need to go." His voice is directive.

"Are your bags ready?"

"Yes, I'm ready," I say to him, as I turn off the computer.

"Savannah has all the information for housesitting?"

"Yes, it's all taken care of."

"Great," Parker says as he grabs my tapestry suitcase. The luggage wheels turn 'round and 'round.

Ha-yoon Jung, Front Desk Manager
The Four Seasons Hotel, Seoul

◆

The luggage wheels turn 'round and 'round. I watch the Americans approach the desk. I am familiar with this look: exhaustion, relief, and a bit of confusion. The woman is dressed smartly in travel clothes, but the back of her hair reveals long hours of sleeping on an airplane. She is too tired to notice or care. No doubt, it has been a long journey for them.

"Good morning! Welcome to The Four Seasons," I say while gently bowing. "May I have your name, please?" I say, while preparing to type the information into the computer.

"Parker and Emma Carter," the man says to me.

I have been expecting their arrival. I was informed, when this reservation was made, to make sure all their needs are met. He is a prestigious American academic and is a keynote speaker for a major psychological conference at the University.

"Dr. Carter, we're so pleased to have you and your wife here. My name is Ha-yoon Jung. I have personally been working with Dr. Chang regarding your accommodations. I think that we have everything in order. The University will be paying for your stay. Would you like to put a credit card on file, in case you have additional charges?

197

Dr. Carter reaches for his wallet and hands me an American Express card. Momentarily, the card catches the light, like a mirror in the sun.

"You are in room number 1212. Our main restaurant opens at 7:00 a.m. and closes at 9:30 p.m." Next to me stands Jiha, a very efficient and polite young man who will have a successful career with The Four Seasons, if he so chooses. I turn to him to clarify instruction.

"당신은 그들의 객실 번호 1212년에 우리의 손님을 도울는가 것입니다."

"This is Jiha. He will help you with your luggage and show you to your room. We hope that you have a wonderful stay here in Seoul. Please don't hesitate to ask for anything that you might need." I hand them the two sliding plastic room keys and bow again. Dr. Carter and his wife bow in return.

Emma Carter

Jiha opens the door to our room and proceeds to turn on the lights and arrange the luggage. This extra dose of thoughtfulness and service is deeply appreciated after such a long trip. The time change and the travel has me physically and emotionally exhausted. I am moving through the world in slow motion. Parker reaches into his wallet for some money. He is unsure of the Korean currency. He holds out some bills. Jiha takes what is appropriate and bows to Parker.

In response, Jiha looks at us and says, "나는 저희를 방문해 당신이 경이로운 시간을 서울에서 보낸ㄴ다는 것을 희망한다."

I have no idea what he just said, but he has a kind face that is authentic and genuine.

Instinctually, we respond to his palpable goodness. Both of us bow and say in unison, "Thank you."

This isn't the kind of hotel that Parker and I stay at. It is not the caliber of hotel that a University typically pays for when hosting visiting academics. It is luxurious, spacious, and last but not least, sexy. Windows grace the eastern view, revealing the vibrancy of the city. There is an Asian flair in the interior design, but it is also international. The bed is glorious: large and welcoming and graced with beautiful natural linens. I feel myself deeply relaxing into my bones. It is a gift to be here and to be welcomed into this foreign land with such grace and generosity.

I close the blackout curtains, and the room is instantly dark. Parker and I quickly take off our clothes and get into bed. I am asleep within seconds. Bidden or unbidden, the dream world takes me.

> I am standing on a picturesque golf course. Although it feels familiar, I know that I am in Korea. It is a beautiful day with a clear, bright blue sky. I am wearing a lovely dress that gently flows in the wind. It feels very feminine. I see my mother at a small, formally set table that sits smack-dab in the middle of the fifth hole. She sees me and calls, "Emma! Emma!" She waves for me to join her. A dog appears to be lying next to her feet. It watches my every move.
>
> I walk over to the table. My mother looks lovely. She is wearing a floral dress with an opulent peach hat that is trimmed in white roses. She is perfectly coiffed and could steal the show from any bride. My mother looks at me. "Darling, where is your hat?"
>
> I sit down at the table. "I'm sorry mother; I forgot it." I feel the familiarity of never being enough and never being the daughter she had hoped for.
>
> My mother looks disappointed. I see words written all over her face, and they say,

"What am I to do with this feral child?" Her unspoken editorial comment is not lost on me.

I notice two yellow birds that sit in a nearby tree. They look at us and tilt their heads as if listening to our conversation.

What appeared from a distance to be a dog is actually a coyote at my mother's feet. She glances down at it. "This dog came up right after I sat down." It looks at my mother and then looks back at me. "Honestly, I think it's been waiting for you."

"Mom, it's not a dog; it's a coyote."

My mother is unfazed. "Is that right?"

"The coyote is a trickster figure," I say to her. It gets up and walks over to me and proceeds to lick my hand. I pet it for a few minutes and then stop. He goes back and lies at the feet of my mother but continues to watch me.

My mother takes the teapot and pours us both a cup of tea. The two yellow birds that had been eavesdropping from a low branch are now singing the most beautiful melody. They are simply enchanting. We are captivated by their magical spell. Both birds then gather some small twigs and leaves and proceed to land on top of my head. They seem to be busy building a nest. I'm not the least bit bothered by it. My mother silently watches, entertained.

The nest creation goes on for some time. A small spider arrives on a twig, and the next thing I know, I have a lovely web veil that gently curves around my face. When the veil is complete, the spider is transported back to the tree. I can feel the weight of my nest hat and their diligent work while they serenade us with their harmonizing song. Meanwhile, the coyote licks his lips as he watches the construction of my hat. His dark eyes dart back and forth, focusing on the movement of the birds.

Both my mother and I are unfazed as we silently drink our tea. And then, all of a sudden, the activity stops. I can feel that the two yellow birds have taken up residency, within the nest, on top of my head.

The coyote whimpers. Saliva drips from his mouth.

My mother looks at me, taking the whole image in. She is amused. "You always were a resourceful child."

I look at her. A deep and painful sadness washes over me like an ocean wave. Powerful emotions well up and then crescent as saltwater tears begin to run down my cheeks. My sadness is profound and old. I struggle to get the words out.

I look at my mother and ask, "What I really need to know is: Do I have character?"

My mother looks at me and respects the gravity of the question. I can see the icy landscape of her heart melting. She reaches up to touch my cheek. The two yellow birds have stopped singing. I feel their bodies shift to the front of the hat, as if poised to listen.

"My darling, beautiful Emma, you always have had character."

Now satisfied, the two yellow birds fly out of the nest and are gone. Simply gone. Leaving us in silence. The void they have left is shocking, and I find myself having to adjust to their absence. I reach up to touch what they have created. I feel the twigs and the leaves and the softness of some moss. And there, exactly in the center of the nest, are two eggs. I take them out of the hat and hold them in the palm of my hand. The tiny eggs are warm, delicate, and ornately speckled.

I wake up alone in the darkened hotel room and slowly grasp where I actually am. I can hear the sound of the shower in the bathroom. I throw off the covers, walk over to the drapes and pull them open. The day is bright, and the whole city moves in a chaotic rhythm. There are pedestrians, buses, bicycles. The foreignness of this place is mesmerizing.

Dr. Chang

Du-na, my younger sister, and I follow the hostess through the dining room. The Four Seasons has an exceptional restaurant in the hotel. I trust that Dr. Carter and his wife are being well cared for. It is a tremendous honor to have him as our keynote speaker for this year's psychological conference. Their trip is twofold, and finding Emma's family eclipsed even my academic priorities.

I recognize Dr. Carter and see that he is with Emma, whom I have yet to meet. They are sitting at a table with a beautiful view of the city. Dr. Carter and his wife are captivated by the view and do not see us walk toward them.

On the opposite side of the room is a black baby grand piano. Two musicians are preparing to play. The man flips through the sheet music on the piano and the woman stands with a violin in her hand.

Du-na and I approach the table. There are two beautifully wrapped gifts sitting on the table. Dr. Carter turns to look at us as we approach and then stands, extending his hand. Emma stands as well.

"Dr. Chang, it is so good to see you!" says Dr. Carter. I reach for his extended hand and at the same time, gently bow.

Dr. Carter turns to his wife. "This is my wife, Emma." Emma is visibly trying to hold back tears. She does not extend her hand or bow. Instead, she takes me in her arms as though we were long-lost friends. "I am so honored to meet you, Dr. Chang."

Emma turns to Du-na. "You must be Du-na! I'm so grateful for all that you have done on our behalf. Words truly fall short." She takes my sister in her arms. This is the American way. Koreans are much more formal, but under the circumstances, it is completely understandable and appropriate. This is the blending of two cultures with an intersection of gratitude. Emma's kindness and gentle spirit is palpable and infectious. Regardless, this will not be an easy conversation.

As if on cue, the musicians begin to play beautiful music. Everyone in the restaurant turns to see where the melody is coming from. For a moment, time stops to appreciate a universal language.

"How lovely! What an unexpected luxury to have music during our dinner," Emma says, glancing in the direction of the musicians.

We each take a seat. Emma gestures to the gifts. "We wanted to get you a little something."

"There was no need for you to get us anything. We are so happy that you're here and that we are able to assist you." As Americans, they may not understand that it is the Korean custom not to open a gift in the presence of the giver. "Du-na and I will enjoy opening our gifts later. I trust that you had good travels and that everything here at the hotel is going well."

"Yes, our flight went without a hitch, and the hotel is absolutely beautiful. They have been very generous to us. We are well cared for. Thank you so much for making these arrangements," says Emma.

I smile at her. "You are welcome. It is an honor to have you both here. If you don't mind, I would prefer you call me by my first name, Hu-na."

Dr. Carter smiles. "That would be nice. My name is Parker. I think it is reasonable for us to move beyond formalities at this point."

"You speak such good English!" says Emma.

"It is true. We speak better English than most people you will find here in Korea. This is because my sister and I went to graduate school in London."

"That's impressive! Graduate school in London, how did that come to be?" asks Emma.

"A friend of our father lived in London. He hosted my sister and I during our time there."

"It was an amazing experience. Both of us go back periodically to visit friends," Du-na offers.

There is a momentary silence. It is hard to know where to begin; there's so much to say. "I am sure Emma is anxious to hear about her family. Why don't we discuss that first, and then we can talk about the conference."

I don't believe Emma would have been so presumptuous, but she is clearly happy with this suggestion.

I turn to look at my sister. "Du-na, why don't you tell them about what you've learned."

"As you know, the biggest break came through my friend, Mi-hee, who owns a shop on Cheju Island. How do you say . . . *synchronistic?*"

We are interrupted by the waitress, who gently bows to all of us. "May I offer you drinks?"

Parker responds, gesturing to himself and Emma. "We will have bottled water." He turns to my sister and I. "Please feel free to have anything that you would like."

"Bottled water will be fine for all of us. Thank you," I offer.

"Very well, thank you." The waitress bows and leaves.

Du-na resumes her story. "Mi-hee, my friend, is familiar with your family. I am happy to escort you to Cheju Island. It will give me an opportunity to see Mi-hee. It will be an advantage to have someone with you who speaks the language. As we move farther away from the city, fewer people speak English. This is my holiday time from work, so it's great timing."

Both Parker and his wife are clearly relieved by my sister's offer. Parker turns to Du-na. "That is gracious of you. We'd like to pay your travel expenses."

"I appreciate the offer, but it's not necessary. I have wanted to go to Cheju Island for some time. I'm honored to help you."

"We will accept your offer, but only if you're absolutely sure. This is a fairly significant gesture."

"I am absolutely sure, Parker."

The waitress walks up and proceeds to serve the bottled water to all of us. "Have you had a chance to look at menu?" she asks.

208

"No, we have not. Why don't you give us a few moments, and then we will order."

The waitress bows and departs.

"In regard to our dinner, since you have never been to Korea, I think it might be best to have a simple meal. Something that might be easy on your stomach."

"I think that's a good idea," Emma says. "What did you have in mind?"

"I was thinking about a fish soup. It's a regional specialty here, and I can only imagine that it would be exceptional at this restaurant."

"That would be lovely. Thank you," says Emma. She quickly glances to her husband with a look that's hard to read.

"Now that that is settled, let's talk about your family, Emma," Du-na offers.

"I can hardly believe this!" Emma offers. "I can't tell you how excited I am. It's hard for me to believe that you were able to locate my family. It's astounding really." Emma pauses, "But I have to tell you, I am slightly bewildered. You never told me exactly who we will be meeting. I understand that some of the villages in Cheju are remote, but I guess I always expected to receive an email or a letter directly from my brother."

My sister and I look at each other. She and I had many discussions that this moment would come. This is Du-na's story to tell.

"I understand. It took some time for us to obtain accurate information. Because you were coming to Korea, both my sister and I felt it was appropriate to tell you this in person." Du-na's hands nervously move over the linen

209

tablecloth as if trying to remove any creases. She glances up at Emma's face, which begins to reveal some anxiety.

"You will be meeting your two young nieces. Sun-ja is seven years old. Mi-ja is four."

The waitress returns to the table. "Are you ready to order your dinner?"

The waitress looks at me. "Yes. We will all have a fish soup. Our guests are from America and are not used to our cuisine. Would you please have the chef use mild spices?"

"Absolutely. Is there anything else at this time?"

"No, that will be all."

The waitress leaves, and an awkward silence returns.

Emma looks confused. *"Two nieces?* I'm sorry. I guess I don't understand. I was expecting to meet my brother and possibly his mother." Emma's anxiety is beginning to rise. Parker's concern is visible as well.

"There's no easy way to say this. You may want to prepare yourself for some sad news." Du-na pauses. "Your brother and his wife were killed just over a year ago in a train accident. In-sook, the mother of your brother and wife of your father, was with them. She was also killed. Your brother, Sang-ho, and his wife were taking In-sook to a doctor in Seoul. The girls stayed with a neighbor."

Emma leans back into her chair. Her left hand goes to her stomach. She tries to contain herself. Parker is working hard to put all the pieces together and understand the ramifications.

"We are very sorry to share such news." I personally feel the depth of their loss. Parker reaches over and tries to comfort Emma. Tears well up in Emma's eyes as she reaches in her purse to find a Kleenex.

"Where are the girls living?" Parker asks.

"The girls are living with their elderly aunt, In-sook's younger sister."

Parker rubs his forehead. "How old is she?"

"She is eighty-one years old."

The reality—*the weight of all of this*—is dawning on Emma and Parker. They look at each other. "What about other family?" Emma asks.

Du-na resumes massaging the linen cloth. "The only other living relative *here* is an uncle. He is eighty-three years old."

"What will happen to the girls when their aunt is too old to care for them?" Emma asks. A hint of hysteria creeps into her voice.

The waitress and an additional server arrive with the food. Beautiful earthenware dishes are set before each of us. The presentation is beautiful, but no one has an appetite.

"Is there anything else that I can bring you?" asks the waitress.

"No. This looks perfect. Thank you so much," Du-na graciously responds.

The waitress bows and leaves.

Parker and Emma look at Du-na, waiting for her answer. "Depending on their financial resources, they will either be sent to a long-term boarding school or to an orphanage. Although this is not my area of social work, I do believe the girls will have a chance for a normal life if they are adopted." Du-na waits a few moments before continuing. "If they are adopted, it is likely that the girls will be separated. Most people want to adopt one child, not two. It will be easier to find a home for Mi-ja, due to her age."

This is too much for Emma. No longer able to conceal her emotions, she chokes back a sob. Emma pushes her chair back and stands up. She is now openly crying. "Please excuse me." She proceeds to leave the restaurant. Parker stands up. "Please excuse us. We'll be back, but it would be best if you go ahead and eat."

Du-na and I watch them leave the restaurant. They pause in the lobby. Emma is doubled over.

"Maybe I should have told her when I first learned the news." Concern and responsibility are visible on my sister's face.

"No, you did the right thing. She may not have come. The hope lies in Emma. This is her family line."

There is a flurry of activity around Emma and her husband. A cluster of people have formed around them. A woman and a man step out of the way to reveal Emma doubled over breathing into a Chanel gift bag.

"Do you think that we should go and help them?" my sister asks.

"No. I think we should give them a bit of room."

"Do you think they will take the girls?"

We both watch the scene in silence as Emma tries to regain her composure.

"It is too soon to tell."

My sister turns to me. "나는 우리가 정당한 일을 했다는 것을 희망한다."

I put my hand over my sister's and feel the weight of her heart. "우리는 맞은 윤리적인 유일한 일을 했다."

212

My attention shifts to the musicians. A woman has joined them and is preparing to sing.

Parker and his wife walk back toward our table. The Chanel bag is now folded and carried by Emma, as if it is a life preserver in a large and overwhelming sea. Neither Du-na nor I have touched our food. Parker pulls out the chair for his wife.

There is a tapping noise as the musicians check the microphone.

Parker Carter
International Psychological Conference in Seoul

The technology assistant taps the temperamental microphone, which just went dead.

The University has a beautiful auditorium. There are probably five hundred people in the audience. Typical of my presentations, there is a high percentage of women. Dr. Chang is at the opposite end of the stage with me. She sits behind a desk and manages the PowerPoint projection. A microphone is also on her desk, should she need to be an interpreter. My speech has been translated into Korean and is projected on a large screen behind me. It is slightly distracting. Although most of these people in the audience speak fluent English, Dr. Chang insisted on the projection.

The technology assistant moves the microphone around, and it begins to work again. He looks at me, bows, and then proceeds to run off the stage.

I take a sip of water and begin again. "Years ago I read a quote, and I have not been able to relocate it or find the source. Nonetheless, I think it's worth repeating: "What we now know is that those countries that disempower women are the most dangerous countries in the world." I pause, to let the quote sink in. "This historical lineage of the masculine—that has had an endless need to dominate and conquer—comes at a high price to the world. War, destruction, terrorism, and technology at our fingertips to do immeasurable damage to the world is not without consequence. Throughout time, the oppression of the feminine has served the masculine." I pause, look into the audience and take a sip of water.

"In the last century, women have made their mark on history: through voting, the demand for equal pay, achieving the appointment of powerful positions in government and in corporations. Medical research alone has changed the trajectory of women by creating various forms of birth control. All the while, the masculine has pursued, as James Hillman articulated, 'a terrible love of war.'"

As I begin to speak, the microphone goes dead yet again. The technical assistant runs back onto the stage and looks embarrassed. I step away from the podium.

Dr. Chang is frustrated and speaks into her microphone. "We're so sorry for this interruption. It may be best if we switch microphones. Why don't we take a five-minute break."

Dr. Chang then speaks in Korean:

"우리는 이 중지를 위해 아주 유감스럽다. 우리가 마이크를 전환하는 경우에 최상 일지도 모른다. 왜 우리가 5 분 쉬지 않는지."

Emma Carter

Du-na and I are sitting directly in front of the stage, three rows back. She has been busy taking notes during Parker's presentation. It is easy for Parker and I to make eye contact. He shoots me a look, veiled in nonjudgment, but I can tell this kind of technical difficulty is hard on his rhythm. Although he has presented in countless conferences, this is quite a different experience and is no doubt challenging.

Du-na turns to me. "This kind of thing makes my sister crazy."

"Yes, I'm sure it does. It's hard on Parker too, but he is experienced enough; he'll be able to adapt."

"Your husband is a very brilliant man."

"Yes, he is. He is also truly a good person. That's what I love most about him."

"My sister tells me he's highly respected in the world of academics."

"I think that depends on whom you're talking to. He has a nontraditional approach to psychology and philosophy; it makes him both loved and despised."

Du-na looks at me, clearly surprised at my honesty. "I understand," she says.

Parker Carter

I step back to the podium and lean into the microphone. "Thank you for your patience." I acknowledge the audience, then take a sip of water and begin again. "As the feminine has evolved, the masculine remains obsessed with oppression and conquering. Now, through technological advancement, we have more power than ever before. Where is our tipping point? *We are facing an endangered planet.* The very sustainability of our world is called into question. Hegel suggested that it may only be in death that our civilization becomes conscious—by truly facing our own annihilation. Is this what is required for us to understand what's at stake?"

I pause to let the question have a presence in the room.

"In closing, I would like to quote my friend and colleague, Dr. Richard Tarnas, 'Perhaps the end of man himself is at hand. But man is not the goal. Man is something that must be overcome and fulfilled, in the embrace of the feminine.'"

I close my notes and lean into the microphone, "Thank you."

There is no applause. The silence is unexpected and jarring. Suddenly, the lights of the auditorium are turned

219

on, which only exacerbates my feelings of scrutiny. Such feminist perspective is difficult enough for the Western mind. I realize these are outrageous ideas for the male-dominated Korean culture. Though it is clear to me that Dr. Chang invited me here to challenge Korean norms, it is difficult to be in this position. I watch the men in the audience look at each other, clearly wondering if they have been bamboozled. The women sit silent, stealing glances to each other with a smile. My backbone works to absorb the damaging impact of the audience. I can feel myself moving into a place of public humiliation.

I take my notes from the podium. Dr. Chang is at the opposite end of the stage and is finalizing the projection of my translated speech. There behind me, on a screen, larger than life, are my words in a foreign language. I look at her and question her judgment of bringing me here. While I will go home to a culture that is more open-minded than this one, she will remain in South Korea.

She looks up at me. In a mere glance, her eyes are warm and compassionate; between she and I, there are a million words in English, in Hindu, in German, in Arabic, in French, in Russian, and Korean. Despite any translation, they say the same thing: we share a world with a concern for its future.

Dr. Chang stands up and moves from behind the protective cover of the desk and walks to the center of the stage. She slowly, humbly, and deeply bows to me. She holds the bow for a prolonged period of time. Clearly, I underestimated her courage as a woman, as an academic, and as a colleague.

220

I am completely stunned by this unexpected act and instinctively glance over to Emma. She looks as shell-shocked as I feel, but then my wife does the most amazing and incredible thing: she stands up and bows to me. As if on cue, Du-na sets down her notes and stands, bowing, next to my wife. In a blanket of silence, one by one, people from the audience stand up and bow to me.

I have been an academic for many years. It has certainly come with its high points and low points to match. There are experiences that are markers in the timeline of my life. I intuitively understand—this moment—*this moment*—will go down as *remarkable*.

I return my notes to the podium. I walk toward Dr. Chang and bow to her. I then turn and bow to the audience. Today, in this place, there is only a silent acknowledgment of what it means to be human and understood.

Emma Carter

It is now 2 a.m., and my patience has worn thin waiting for Parker to return to the hotel. After his presentation, Duna suggested we go shopping. This was an offer I could not resist and allowed Parker to attend to his professional obligations.

Seoul is an amazing city, and it was a gift to have Duna as my guide. Over the last several months I have done significant research on South Korea, its culture, Korean etiquette, and history. I have read about the markets and was hoping to visit one.

We made a beeline to the Dongdaemun Marketplace, which is the heart of the fashion district. It was amazing. Nothing could have prepared me for the vibrancy of this place. I felt like I was on a double latte high in the glorious land of shopping! I found a variety of small gifts to take home. There was a wide range of ages in the shop owners; many appeared to be well over seventy. Anything I could ever have wanted was here: bolts of colorful fabric, shoes, purses, fashionable clothing, tailored coats, and last but certainly not least, beautiful négligées.

There are many ways to a man's heart, and after Parker's presentation, I had my mind set on a memorable seduction. The black négligée I purchased was made of silk, with tiny spaghetti straps. What makes it unique is the massive embroidery and peekaboo netting that cascades down the front. It was a worthy investment that will honor this memory for years to come.

But now I sit here, "all dressed up, with nowhere to go." The thrill of my intention and plans dwindled three hours ago. I have occupied my time by writing postcards and rereading the tourist book of Cheju Island.

My growing disappointment is interrupted by the sound of two men coming down the hallway. They are loud, boisterous, happy, and clearly drunk. I recognize the voice of my husband. I hear him struggle at the door with the key. I get up to open the door for him, discreetly standing behind it. Instead of acknowledging me, Parker speaks to his partner in crime in a loud and drunken swagger, "I expect to see you in Santa Barbara!"

Parker struts into the hotel room. His tie is loose, and the top button of his shirt is undone. He glances at me, dressed-up in a gift. I quickly shut the door as he proceeds to do a skilled, suave pelvis rotation worthy of John Travolta's talents. He is drunk and ready for love.

I look at him both bewildered and amused. "Good god, you're really drunk!"

"Yes I am," he responds with a dose of pride. "Male bonding honey—Korean style—and I like it!"

He dances over to me and reaches for my hand. With an artful, experienced swing step, he throws me away from him. Our hands remain locked. Like a rubber band, I snap back into his embrace. Despite his inebriation, he has a reasonable sense of balance. It's been a while, but in the old days, Fred Astaire and Ginger Rogers didn't have anything on us. Parker holds me tightly with my back arched over. He looks intently into my eyes. "You got my message that I was going out with the guys." It was more of a statement than a question.

"Yes, I did, thank you."

He proceeds to twirl me around the room in an experienced two-step. With his arm around my back, our bodies are melded together, tighter than we need to be.

Again, he pauses to make a point, suspending me in his arms, eyes locked with mine. "We're going to have a house full of Koreans next year."

"We are?"

"Yes," he responds.

Satisfied, he twirls me back to the chair and plants a kiss on my lips. He plops down on the bed and struggles to take off his jacket.

"Is there a place to sing karaoke in Santa Barbara?"

I wince at the thought of this. "Did you sing karaoke?"

"As a matter of fact, I did."

I can only imagine the look of this, and I can't help but be both embarrassed for him and entertained.

As if on cue, Parker breaks out in song, "Somewhere over the rainbow, way up high." Suddenly he stops and looks at me really seriously. "Honestly honey, I think I have a future."

"May I recommend that you keep your day job?" I see his face drop just a little, so I quickly add, "Just for now." Evidently, too much liquor comes with delusions. "That was an interesting song choice," I say to him.

"It was that, or Gloria Gaynor's 'I Will Survive.'"

"No Barry White?"

Parker looks deeply disappointed, realizing his lost opportunity.

"No. No Barry White."

That was a loss, I think to myself. Parker lies back on the bed and puts his head on the pillow. Clearly, he needs assistance. I proceed to take off his shoes. If he did this on a regular basis, I'd have some serious concerns. I have no doubt that he needed an outlet after his presentation, and just like I had my dose of Korean culture with Du-na, he should have the same liberty.

"I made some *really good friends!*" He looks at me swooning. I am struck by the songbirds of love that are tweeting over his head.

"You look entirely too happy," I say, suspicion creeping into my voice. "Did they take you to a gisaeng house?"

Parker looks stunned—busted—guilty. "*How did you know?!*"

As if on cue, I stop rubbing his feet. "I read about them in the tour book. A gisaeng is like a Japanese geisha."

"They're *companions, skilled in the art of conversation,*" Parker says defensively.

"Did you have *a companion,* honey?" I try not to be pissed.

"Well . . . aaaaahhhhhh . . . yeah. She came to me. *Really!*" Egg is clearly visible on his face.

"I bet she did."

With the cat out of the bag, he can't stop himself. "She was *f a s c i n a t e d* by my research. She was *b e a u t i f u l* and brilliant." He appears to be reliving the cherished memories of the evening. "She was exceptional."

Parker should've stopped while he was behind.

"Think of it as my small contribution to international relations." A large hiccup escapes him.

"I've no doubt you made significant inroads to political healing."

Parker looks at me sweetly. "I knew you would understand. Could you rub my feet some more?"

"No, sweetheart, I'm done rubbing your feet."

He looks wounded and disappointed.

"Did you forget we have an hour-long flight tomorrow to Cheju Island?" I ask.

He begins a deep and primal moaning. "*Oh god, did you need to remind me?*"

"Evidently, I did."

Parker closes his eyes and begins to snore immediately. I leave him fully clothed on the bed. I'm too agitated to sleep, so I pick up the tour book for Cheju Island. On the cover of the book is an aerial photograph of the island.

Emma Carter

We stand in a cluster of Koreans ready to board Korean Air for our flight to Cheju Island. As passengers board the plane, their tickets are checked and their troubles are left behind. Smiles are exchanged and hands are held; even crying babies seem to take on a different energy. Cheju Island is known as the honeymoon island of South Korea, which means that happiness is everywhere. Everywhere, that is, except on my husband's face, which is a pale shade of green. He wears dark sunglasses to buffer himself from the world.

    Parker, Du-na, and I find our seats on the small aircraft. There is the traditional shuffle of people organizing the overhead bins, getting out their novels or magazines. Due to his height, Parker always takes the aisle seat, and I am by the window. Du-na is across from us on the aisle. With everyone settled and their seatbelts fastened, the airplane begins to back away from the terminal. The stewardess speaks in Korean, gesturing the international language of seatbelt use, lighting along the floor, the exit doors and the use of oxygen masks. She then sits down and fastens her seatbelt.

    Parker rests his head against the seat back and closes his eyes, still wearing his sunglasses. I can tell that he's bracing for the plane's takeoff.

Now on the tarmac and poised in position, the plane begins to accelerate. The front of the plane goes up, the wheels gently lift off the ground, and the nose of the airplane steeply climbs into the sky. This is not good for Parker. He quickly searches for the vomit bag and holds it on his lap. The plane slowly attains its altitude goal and becomes horizontal again. After a few moments, the seatbelt light goes off, and the stewardess begins the preparation for the beverage service.

Parker returns the vomit bag to its proper place, unfastens the seatbelt, and quickly departs to the bathroom. He barely gets the door shut before vomiting can clearly be heard by everyone. Passengers exchange sympathetic glances.

I lean toward Du-na. "He is no match for your sister's colleagues."

"Evidently not. Few Americans would be."

Within a few minutes, he returns, dabbing the sides of his mouth.

I look at my husband. "Are you okay?"

"Maybe when I get off this plane."

I know better than this, but the truth is, memories of last night are tainting my experience of today. This is our only chance of having a private conversation before we meet my family. "How beautiful was she?"

"Who?"

"The gisaeng."

This line of questioning isn't helping Parker's hangover. "What are you talking about?" He sounds irritable.

230

"The gisaeng from last night, *your companion.* The one who was beautiful and brilliant. *So brilliant!*

"Did I say that?"

"Yes."

"I guess that explains why I was sleeping on the bed fully clothed."

"That would be a clue."

Parker bends over. I can't help but wonder if he's going to vomit again. His voice is flat and obligatory. He whispers to me, "She wasn't as pretty or brilliant as you. Does that help?"

I am unimpressed and hurt. "Under the circumstances, it will do."

Silence lingers between us. We both close our eyes for the remainder of the flight, each of us, trying to find a bit of personal space.

Oblivious to passing time, we are jarred back to reality by the stewardess announcing our arrival at Cheju. The airplane circles around the island and gives us a priceless aerial view of this beautiful place. The water is a bright topaz blue. The terrain varies and is accented by ample mountains. Billowing white clouds dot the blue sky. This is a moment that will be forever etched in my mind. Everything I have known in the past, about who I am, about my life, and how I have defined my family will be forever changed with this trip. I am literally stepping through a portal. In my wildest dreams, I could never have imagined *this.*

231

The Ancestors

It is about three o'clock in the afternoon when Parker, Emma, and Du-na prepare to exit the airplane, carry-on luggage in tow. Most of the passengers stand lingering, balancing all their belongings, waiting for the airplane door to open. There are also couples on the airplane who linger back. There is no need to rush forward; they are not meeting family or friends. They have come to Cheju on their honeymoon. They are here only to find each other.

Passengers leave the plane and exit the jet bridge, negotiating their luggage. A cluster of people have gathered in the main terminal and stand anxiously waiting behind the appropriate parameter. Enthusiastic waves are exchanged. Du-na searches the crowd of people and makes eye contact with her friend, Mi-hee. They wave to each other with excitement.

Du-na turns to Emma. "Do you see the woman in the bright blue dress?

"Yes, I see her," Emma answers.

"That is my friend, Mi-hee."

Emma waves to her with the same enthusiasm that Du-na has. "She looks lovely. I'm so excited to meet her," Emma says.

In the terminal, families with children organize themselves, while the elderly slowly find their balance. Du-na and Mi-hee embrace each other, with an exchange of tears and laughter. "나는 당신을 보게 아주 행복하다! 당신은 환상적인Mi hee 를 본다! 당신은 어떻게 아주 젊습니 까 체재하는가," Du-na says to Mi-hee.

Mi-hee laughs, wiping away her tears. Rapid and emotional Korean follows, "그것은 너 무 길다 계속 나의 친애하는 친구. 당신은 아주 아름답고 아주 행복하게 본다. 나는 들리기 위 여위에 들어가고 있는 무슨이에 관하여 당신의 생활에서 기다릴 수 없다. 나는 아주 기 쁘다당신 여기에서 있다."

Meanwhile, Parker and Emma witness the reunion. Du-na turns to them. "I would like you to meet my friend, Mi-hee."

Mi-hee bows. "English, not so good." Mi-hee breaks into a peal of laughter. "Happy to meet you. Happy you here."

Emma and Parker bow in return. "We are happy to meet you, and our Korean, not so good!" says Emma. Mi-hee and Du-na continue to laugh like two schoolgirls. Emma reaches into her carry-on and produces a wrapped gift for Mi-hee. "This is a small gesture of our appreciation, for everything you have done for us." Emma tries a bit of Korean, "당신을 아주 많이 감사하십시오." Mi-hee smiles broadly and accepts the gift. "You welcome. So honor to help you find family. Very special for me."

Tears spring to Emma's eyes. "Very special for us."

"Yes, very special for us," Mi-hee says, nodding her head in agreement.

Mi-hee and Du-na lead the way to the baggage claim while talking nonstop in Korean. Emma and Parker take in their surroundings and try to get their bearings. Parker strives to regain his color.

The luggage makes its debut on the carousel. With a quick inventory of the two foreign travelers, Mi-hee takes the handle of Emma's luggage. "I help you to car."

"Thank you so much, Mi-hee," Emma responds.

It is a beautiful summer day, with humidity that is intense and invasive. Mi-hee's car is tiny and sporty. Emma and Parker's luggage barely fits in the trunk. Parker wipes the sweat off his face as they get settled into the back seat of the hot car. Mi-hee gets in behind the wheel and Du-na settles into the passenger seat, arranging her carry-on between her feet. Momentarily, Du-na stops her Korean chatter and turns to Emma and Parker in the back seat. "We will go to the eastern side of Cheju Island. Your family lives about thirty minutes from here."

"Okay, that sounds great," says Emma while she ties her hair in a ponytail to get it off her neck.

Despite the heat, there is an aloof coolness between Emma and Parker.

Mi-hee starts the car and exits the parking lot. With the car windows down, the breeze brings a welcome relief, and the salty smell of the ocean surrounds them.

Again Du-na turns around in the seat to face Emma and Parker. "Your family lives by Songsan Ilchulbong, which is an extinct volcano. I will be staying with Mi-hee. She is about twenty minutes from the children."

Parker leans forward, grabbing the back of the seat, and speaks to both Mi-hee and Du-na, "Thank you.

Thank you for everything." His sincerity is palpable. In acknowledgment, Du-na smiles and momentarily puts her hand over his.

The conversation resumes in Korean between Mi-hee and Du-na, periodically interrupted by dramatic responses, knee slapping, and laughter. It is a look of friendship, old friendship, with years of commitment.

Through the back window, the beauty of this foreign place parades its unique culture. A group of children play on the side of the road. When they see the white faces of Emma and Parker, they wave and yell at the passing car. Two of the children laugh as they chase the car. Emma turns around and waves to them out the back window. A man walks next to the road with a whole fish suspended through the gills by bamboo. Old rusted bicycles share the road with contemporary vehicles. Colorful open markets sell vegetables and fruit alongside fish markets. There are many people walking and carrying groceries in patterned cotton backpacks. The sights, sounds, and smells are gloriously stunning.

Parker reaches his hand across the void to Emma. She turns to look at him. He takes her hand and kisses it, a gesture of peace offering. She looks at him with contemplation. She kisses his hand in return. Offer accepted.

The tiny car makes its way along the winding road. The harbor city is left behind and quickly gives way to small family farms that are scattered along the road and hillside. The homes have a captivating architectural design and have similarity to both Chinese and Japanese aesthetics. Some have clay roofs of tile, others have straw roofs. There are open fields, livestock, and groves of fruit trees, carefully aligned and spaced.

With sheer exhaustion, Parker closes his eyes and tips his head back into the headrest. He is quickly dozing. Emma, on the other hand, is wide awake.

Finally, Mi-hee slows the car and turns left onto a dirt road. The road ascends up rolling hills until it comes to an ornate home surrounded by tangerine trees. The house reflects a traditional design with a straw roof and clay walls. A low stone wall surrounds the house, creating a front courtyard. In its simplicity, it is utterly exquisite. In addition, it is impeccably kept, which elicits a quality of serenity and stillness.

Emma gently touches Parker's knee. "Wake up, honey, we're here."

Parker opens his eyes and rubs his face. He looks out the window to the house. On one side is a garden with growing vegetables; on the other side is a large chicken coop, big enough to stand in. Inside the chicken coop, a little girl scatters seeds for the chickens.

An elderly woman is in the garden with the younger child. All three stop what they are doing and look to the car. The older girl exits the cage and wipes her hands on her clothes. Min-sook, the elderly aunt, yells in Korean, "그들은 여기 있다! 그들은 여기 있다! 빨리 소녀는집에, 당신이 볼품있다 그래야 가고 당신을 청소되어 얻자!" All three quickly move to the house.

"She wants the girls to be clean and presentable for you. They will be out in a moment."

All four get out of the car and patiently stand, waiting for the front door to open. The summer katydids are in full song; the chorus is everywhere. The warm tropical breeze rustles the leaves. Culture shock is visible on the faces of Emma and Parker. Emma begins to rub her stomach, an unconscious ramification of growing anxiety. The humidity doesn't help.

The front door of the house opens. Min-sook has the hand of Mi-ja, the youngest daughter. The older daughter, Sun-ja, follows. All three are dressed in traditional Korean attire called chima jeogori. Typically, these dresses are saved for festivals or special occasions. The colors are bright and beautiful, and all three of them are a sight to behold. The two little girls stand straight, like dutiful soldiers.

Mi-hee breaks the ice; she bows in greeting, "여보세요 분 In-sook, 일요일 Sun-ja, 및 Mi-ja, 나는 Emma, 와 Parker, 를 데려왔다."

Min-sook, Sun-ja, and Mi-ja bow to the American guests. Emma and Parker bow in return. Du-na has been coaching Emma in small phrases of Korean. Emma has practiced for this moment, "우리는 당신을 만나게 아주 행복하다."

A delight spreads across the face of the elderly aunt. She addresses the two young girls, "당신은, 당신의 아름다운 아줌마 이미 말한다 한국어를 본다!" She looks to Emma, smiles and bows. "우리는 당신이 있기 위하여 여기에서 명예를 준다."

Du-na turns to Emma and Parker. "She welcomes you to her home. They are so happy that you are here. They are very honored to have you as their guests."

"Please tell her we are honored to be here," Emma responds.

"그들은 여기 있기 위하여 명예를 주고 말하기 위하여 당신을 감사하십시오," Du-na says.

The two little girls silently watch the exchange between the adults. They are tall, beautiful children with a hint of Norwegian heritage showing through. Freckles are sprinkled across their nose and cheeks. A bit of dirt remains on the face of Sun-ja.

Min-sook looks oddly, hauntingly, familiar to Emma and Parker. Min-sook smiles broadly, revealing a missing side tooth. Sun-ja smiles as well. Ironically, she is missing the same exact tooth. To see them smiling next to each other is comical.

The wheels of recognition turn for Parker and Emma. Almost simultaneously they recognize Min-sook from the Korean restaurant. She was the elderly hostess. The reality of this hits them both at the same time. They are speechless. Emma's world begins to spin. She begins to sway from side to side. Then her knees buckle beneath her as she faints. Parker quickly grabs one side of her while Du-na grabs the other. Together, they try to stabilize her. Parker then picks her up and carries her in his arms. Min-sook briskly leads the way through the courtyard.

Parker assertively asks Du-na, "Please ask Min-sook if she has ever been to America."

This seems like a very odd question to Du-na, given the circumstances, but she directs the question to her nonetheless. The two women converse in Korean.

"No, she has never been to America."

Dissatisfied, Parker continues the questioning. "Please ask her if we've ever met."

239

Again, the two women carry on a conversation in Korean. As they approach the house, a snake, coiled up, lies next to the shrubs. It lifts its head to watch the chaotic parade. The snake goes unnoticed. This conversation takes significantly longer than the first.

Du-na translates. "She met both of you in a dream. In the dream she was in America, and you both were eating Korean food. She felt the dream was a good omen. In-sook was in the dream as well but as a young woman."

Min-sook opens the front door to the house. The snake goes up a tree with branches that touch the house and it silently disappears into the straw roof. The house interior reflects the simplistic beauty of the architecture. It has very open floor plan, with the kitchen off to one side and the living room and the dining room in one large space. Min-sook quickly takes a futon out of a cabinet and puts it on the floor for Emma. Parker lays Emma down.

Min-sook continues to talk to Du-na. Void of any judgment, Du-na carefully and respectfully listens, then turns to Parker. "She has good memories of you both from that first meeting. She is wondering if Emma still has trouble with coughing. If so, she may have something for her."

Min-sook leaves the room. The back door slams. Parker kneels next to his wife and gently moves a stray hair out of Emma's face. Sun-ja and Mi-ja watch while sitting on the floor. Du-na and Mi-hee stand on one side.

Sun-ja, the oldest daughter, says to Parker. "She is very pretty."

Parker is stunned. "You speak English?"

"Daddy and Grandma In-sook both spoke fluent English. They taught English to Mi-ja and I. Mi-ja was young. She has probably forgotten most of it by now."

She turns to her little sister. "Have you forgotten all the English Daddy taught us?

Mi-ja smiles. "No!" It appears this may be the only word she remembers.

The back door opens. Min-sook returns with a wrapped bundle of dried herbs. She lights the herbs by the burning embers of the kitchen woodstove. The smoke surrounds her, and a pungent smell begins to fill the house. Min-sook blows out the flame, walks over to Emma and gently waves the smoldering herbs under her nose. Almost instantly, Emma's eyes open. Emma looks up to see smiling faces, some with more teeth than others.

Min-sook says something in Korean to Sun-ja.

Sun-ja instructs Emma, "You are to remain lying down. Auntie will make tea and serve food."

Emma looks astonished. "You speak English?!"

"Yes, I learned from Daddy and Grandma In-sook. We also have English classes at school starting in the third grade."

Du-na lets out a sigh of relief. "I can see you will be just fine here. Mi-hee and I will go now and return Thursday morning to get you around nine o'clock. That will give us two hours until the plane leaves."

"That sounds good. Thank you. We need to get the luggage out of the car," says Parker.

Sun-ja, who was next to Emma on her knees, now springs to her feet, looking to Parker and ready to please. "I can help!"

241

The four exit the living room, leaving Mi-ja, the youngest daughter, by Emma. Conversation takes place between the elderly aunt and Mi-ja. Clearly, some instruction has happened. Min-sook returns to the wood-burning stove and resumes cooking. As her newly appointed caretaker, Mi-ja carefully examines Emma. Mi-ja is captivated by Emma's hair and reaches out to feel it. She then touches Emma's face . Emma watches her, taking in the fact that this child is her brother's child—her niece. The reality sinks in that she had a brother she will never know and a whole family history—unexperienced—until this moment.

A tear forms in Emma's eye and rolls down her cheek. Mi-ja catches Emma's tear with her finger, as if capturing a falling star, and puts it under her own eye, as if it were her tear. The tear rolls down Mi-ja's cheek. Emma and Mi-ja smile at each other and then begin to laugh. Emma reaches out and tickles Mi-ja, who bursts into giggles.

The sound of Mi-hee's car leaving can be heard. The front door opens, and Sun-ja comes dancing in, like a twirling dervish, followed by Parker. Parker has a small, beautifully wrapped gift he presents to Min-sook. She bows in gratitude. Parker bows in return. The gift is set on the table, left unopened.

Parker returns to Emma and drops to his knees to talk to her. "I think you'll be quite pleased with our accommodations. Evidently your brother, Sang-ho, was a renowned architect and specialized in "hanok," which is architecture that honors traditional Korean homes. One of his first projects was to build Min-sook a guesthouse in the backyard. We are staying there."

Parker takes a breath and smiles to Emma. "Honestly, honey, it's extraordinary, and it comes complete with a falcon."

"A falcon? How did Min-sook get a falcon?"

Sun-ja speaks directly to Emma. "Daddy brought it here from the mainland. Auntie has had it all my life. Something is wrong with the wing."

The conversation is interrupted by a knock at the front door. Min-sook goes to the door. Happy, rapid Korean is spoken. She bows in gratitude to the visitor and takes a large plate. Min-sook returns with a beautiful presentation of fresh oysters. There is a shared appreciation for the impressive gift. She then places it on the low wooden dining room table that is surrounded by floor pillows. Min-sook instructs Sun-ja to have Emma and Parker come to the table.

Emma slowly begins to sit up, and Parker helps her to regain her balance. The two young girls take their place on the floor pillows. Parker helps Emma to delicately move across the wooden floor and join the others on the cushions. Min-sook pours the tea and serves the spicy fish stew out of a large cast-iron pot. Min-sook speaks to Sun-ja, clearly with more instruction.

"Auntie hopes that Emma will enjoy the fish stew. Right now, fish is better for her than land meat." Parker and Emma glance at each other.

Emma's color returns, along with her spark and energy. The dinner is divine. Steam from the large pot swirls and floats over the table with an exquisite aroma. Everyone eats in silence. Min-sook looks at Emma with a smile from ear to ear, and in that simple gesture, the international language of welcome is spoken.

When the meal is finished, Min-sook rises and walks over to an altar, which is clearly visible from the table. The shrine has a beautiful golden Buddha, framed photos of people, a fresh flower, rice, fruit, and lit candles. Min-sook gets down on her knees and bows in prayer. She then picks up the small, ornate bowl of rice grains.

Hidden between the layers of straw on the roof, the snake watches.

Min-sook comes over to Emma and gestures that she should hold out her hands. Emma cups the palms of her hands. Min-sook stirs the rice with her index finger, then removes a pinch of grains and puts these into Emma's cupped hands. Min-sook places her aged hands over Emma's, and again appears to be in prayer. She gestures that Emma should shake her hands with the palms closed. This done, Min-sook gently opens Emma's hands to reveal the distribution of the rice. The kernels are scattered, but in the absolute center of Emma's right palm are four kernels together. Min-sook gasps in delight. The eighty-year-old woman is filled with immense joy and appears to suddenly be years younger. Laughing, she reaches over to kiss Emma, then Parker, then the two girls, all the while rapidly speaking in Korean. She gets up and goes back to the altar and falls to her knees, speaking in Korean.

"What just happened?" asks Emma.

"She just read your fortune," offers Sun-ja.

"Do you know what she is so happy about?"

"The ancestors say you are a person of solid character. Your destiny is unfolding."

"Which is?"

244

"She didn't say. Right now it is between her, the ancestors, and the gods and goddess."

Parker and Emma look at each other. In their silence, words are clearly visible: Is their destiny the acquisition of two children?

Min-sook gets up and speaks to Sun-ja. Min-sook bows and leaves the house.

"Auntie is going to the village temple. We will stay here with you," says Sun-ja. "Mi-ja and I need to do something, but we will be right back."

Sun-ja speaks in Korean to her younger sister. Sun-ja takes Mi-ja's hand and takes a lantern off a small wooden table. The lantern is beautiful. The wood has been hand carved and is very ornate, and it is lined with handmade paper. The two children leave the house.

With dusk approaching, the quality of light within the home is beginning to change to a beautiful peach glow. The lit candles on the altar become increasingly prominent.

Now alone, Emma and Parker each begin to speak at the same time. Parker gestures for Emma to speak first. Emma seizes the opportunity to talk.

"Once upon a time, I was a stable woman, predictable, maybe even a bit boring. Next thing I know, I'm hyperventilating in a Chanel gift bag in a hotel lobby halfway around the world and passing out in the street." Emma briefly pauses for a breath. "I thought Min-sook was the hostess from the restaurant, but of course that can't be. Doesn't this concern you? It concerns me."

"I'm not sure what to make of all this, either."

"What were you going to say to me?" Emma asks.

245

Parker looks over to the altar, to the photos of the ancestors. He gets up and walks over to it. Clearly he sees something.

"It can wait," he says, speaking to the photos.

Emma sees what he is looking at. She gets up and joins him. They both stand before the altar, looking at one specific photo. The photo is of In-sook as an old woman, Emma's brother, Sang-ho, who appears to be in his late forties, and Emma's father. The photo isn't that old. They appear to be one happy family.

"Oh, my god . . . that's my father!"

Emma takes a step forward. Her right foot lands in the middle of an emotional snare. She is quickly inverted, emotionally hanging upside-down, suspended—netless, once again flailing. She bends over and tries to breathe. "How can this be? I can't take much more. You're the professional. What's the reasonable reaction to all this?" she says, speaking to the floor.

"I honestly don't know. We moved beyond reasonable some time ago ."

The girls are laughing outside, and it is easy to hear them approaching the house. Sun-ja calls to Emma and Parker through the screen door. "We have a present for you! Close eyes. No peeking!"

Emma slowly stands up and collects herself. Emma and Parker turn around and do as they are told. There is quiet whispering in Korean between the two girls, as if whispering a foreign language would make a difference to Emma and Parker. Sun-ja hands the lantern to her younger sister to present. The lantern is now filled with fireflies. Their magical glow turns on and off. An exquisite

246

wonder has been captured, like shadow puppets, behind a handmade paper curtain.

Mi-ja holds the lantern straight out with pride written all over her face.

"Open eyes!" demands Sun-ja.

Emma and Parker open their eyes and stand speechless. The two girls, with sparkling eyes and big smiles, are a sight to behold. Emma and Parker go down on their knees to be the same height. Mi-ja holds out the lantern for them to take. Parker gestures that Emma should receive the gift.

"Thank you. This is so lovely," says Emma.

"Daddy made the lantern. It is very old. He made it when he was young," says Sun-ja.

"We are so sorry about the loss of your mother and father and your grandmother. How are you both doing?" Emma asks, her voice strained with emotion.

Sun-ja speaks in Korean to Mi-ja, now the appointed interpreter for her little sister.

"Mi-ja never cried. I cried a lot. Auntie helped their spirits to leave the world." Sun-ja gestures to the lantern. "We need to take you to your room before the bugs stop."

"Yes, yes, of course," Emma responds.

The two girls lead the way out the back of the house to a stunningly beautiful backyard with rolling hills and old-growth trees. Behind the house are large ceramic pots with lids. Emma turns to Parker, "Those must be for storing kimchee."

"Let me guess, the tour book?"

"Exactly," Emma smiles.

247

They walk away from the house, and in those few steps, they enter another world, more wild and untamed. Emma hands Parker the lantern, and he holds it up, as if to illuminate the way. Nestled among the trees is an ornate cottage with a red tile roof that gently curves up in each corner. The roof is like a stunning hat that ever so gently landed on the dwelling. A porch graces the front of the house. It is clear: this home was built by an artist. It is also likely, this same artist had a hand in the beauty of Min-sook's home. In the front yard is an old tree whose branches extend far and wide. There, on a low-hanging bare branch, is a falcon tethered by one foot. The bird watches their every move. At the door, the girls say goodnight, bow, and go back to the main house.

Parker opens the door for Emma. The one-room dwelling has an exotic interior, simple, and inviting. A golden statue of Buddha, sitting in a lotus blossom, graces the back wall. Candles are lit around the statue. It is calming to observe such serene beauty. A futon has been put on the floor for them. They step into grace.

Emma walks to the window and opens the screen. They lean against the open sill. Parker holds up the lantern. Emma's hand carefully lifts the latch of the lantern and opens the door. The fireflies, like wishes, like blessings, fly out of the lantern. They disperse throughout the backyard. Parker and Emma absorb the experience in silence.

Parker looks at Emma. "I didn't have a chance to tell you. You bowing at the conference, that gesture . . . that gesture meant the world to me."

248

Emma smiles at Parker. His hands gently release her ponytail, and her hair falls loosely over her shoulders. Emma turns her body into his. He wraps his arms around her, pulls her to him and kisses her. A few random fireflies are loose within the room; like a sensuous Morse code, they speak unspoken words.

Inside the guesthouse, it is 4:00 a.m. and Emma and Parker are asleep. The door slowly opens. It is Min-sook; she is holding a lantern that lights the small room. She proceeds to gently nudge them, speaking softly in Korean. Sun-ja enters the room, wiping her eyes as if trying to wake up herself.

Sun-ja whispers, "Time to get up. We are going to climb Songsan to watch the sunrise. Min-sook has tea ready. Our ride will be here soon."

Sun-ja and Min-sook then depart, leaving the lit lantern in the room.

"What the hell . . ." groans Parker.

Emma responds, in a dreamlike state, "I read about it. It's a bit of a hike."

"You and the tour book."

Emma gets up. By the light of the lantern she puts on her clothes. She adds some energy bars and a few bottles of water to a backpack. Parker falls back asleep.

"Parker, honey, wake up. You need to get dressed."

"Can't you go without me?"

"No. You won't want to miss this. It'll be worth it."

Begrudgingly, he gets up.

All five stand on the dirt road in front of Min-sook's house. Emma and Parker look like true Americans; they each wear Nike walking shoes, and Parker has on a baseball cap. Emma wears a brimmed hat. By the light of the moon, she compulsively rubs sunscreen on her face and arms. A digital camera hangs over her shoulder. Min-sook has packed a picnic breakfast, which is in a large straw shoulder bag that Parker is prepared to carry.

A small car rounds the corner. A woman, as old as Min-sook, pulls up in front of them. She gets out of the car. Korean is spoken between Min-sook and her friend. The friend looks at Emma and Parker, bows and says her name, pronouncing it for the Americans, "Eun-hee Koh."

Emma and Parker bow in return, "Emma and Parker."

With quick greetings exchanged, Eun-hee returns to the driver's seat while Min-sook gets in next to her friend. The remaining four pile in the back seat like sardines. Sun-ja sits between Emma and Parker, Mi-ja rides on Parker's lap. She leans her head against his chest and falls asleep. Emma watches this interaction and smiles at Parker. Before long, all four are asleep in the back seat, their bodies molded together like contortionists. The sky remains dark as the car moves along the quiet road.

Eun-hee pulls into a parking area at the trailhead. Everyone piles out of the car and finds the path in the dark dawn. The two younger sisters run ahead, laughing. Emma and Parker walk in silence. The older Korean women visit in their own language. The trail climbs. The view changes with the elevation, and the sky grows a little lighter.

Eventually, the children slow their pace and join Emma and Parker. Mi-ja wants to hold Parker's hand.

250

It is a significant walk for a four-year old, although she does not complain. The sky begins to blush with the approaching dawn. They are now able to see the town below and the awakening community.

They slowly approach the summit. Both Emma and Parker are feeling their age, while the two elderly women don't even break a sweat. Emma turns to Sun-ja, "How is it that those two women can do this hike so easily?

Sun-ja smiles proudly. "They were haenyo divers. They only quit last year, because they said they were getting too old."

Emma turns to Parker, "I read about them in the tour book. They have tremendous lung capacity and dive without an air tank. Haenyo divers played a really important role by providing food, because rice doesn't grow on this island. Culturally, this also resulted in women having a fair amount of power."

Sun-ja smiles at Emma. Parker refrains from commenting.

"Have you done this walk many times, Sun-ja?" asks Emma.

"Yes, many times with my parents and every summer with Grandma and Grandpa."

Sun-ja's answer hits Emma like a brick. "Which grandparents?"

"Grandma In-sook and Grandpa Randall."

Emma is stunned and stops. She takes a sip of water. Sun-ja continues, not realizing that Earth has stopped turning for Emma. "When I was a little girl Daddy would carry me in a backpack."

251

The summit is clearly visible. Min-sook turns back, looking at the four of them, and speaks in Korean, giving instruction.

"The sun is going to come up. We are almost there. Auntie would like us to keep walking.

They begin to walk again in silence. Meanwhile, Parker gestures to Mi-ja that she should now hold Emma's hand. Mi-ja takes Emma's hand.

They round the bend to the summit of Mount Songsan Ilchulbong. The sky is a warm peach. The view is spectacular!. They are on top of the world. The ocean is a beautiful topaz blue; the color of blue varies with the depth of the water. Small fishing boats exit the harbor, leaving a gentle wake behind them. Birds congregate around the harbor, a few of them follow the boats out to sea. Both Emma and Parker are awestruck by the sheer beauty.

On the top of the summit, there is an open, flat grassy area. Min-sook removes a cotton spread from the straw shoulder bag and lays it on the ground. She gestures to Emma and Parker to sit. Min-sook speaks in Korean.

Off to one side, Min-sook, Eun-hee, Sun-ja, and Mi-ja stand in preparation. Emma and Parker sit watching them. Min-sook and Eun-hee move in perfect unison, like mirrored images of each other. They appear to be doing a form of tai chi. Their gentle hand movements summon the sun itself. The two young girls join in; their tiny bodies reflect two great masters. The vibrant elderly and the innocent young are gently seducing the dawn. The sun is beckoned, and a tip of orange peeks over the ocean. Slowly and peacefully, it makes its debut. When fully up, Min-sook speaks to the sun in Korean. All four stop

252

and bow deeply, honoring its blessing. Parker and Emma applaud and cheer their efforts. They stand and also bow to the sun.

Min-sook unpacks the breakfast, complete with tea. They sit, eating in silence, enjoying the beauty and experience of such a place. Steam rises from their picnic cups.

Randall J. Lawrence

I stopped having the nightmares—the ones where I was drowning while surrounded by life rafts. I was an old man when I finally had the courage to swim to the dock and take In-sooks's extended hand. By then, my son, Sang-ho, was a grown adult. I didn't abate all of my responsibilities. I had sent money to In-sook to care for him. Year after year, she saved the money. By the time he was a young man, there was enough savings to send him to a prestigious college.

No apology can make amends for leaving her pregnant. My behavior simply was not forgivable, not by a priest, perhaps not even by God himself. The only amends that I could make was to be present to the best of my ability. By this time I had a wife—a different wife—well, I'd had a number of wives since In-sook. I had responsibilities in the United States.

In-sook and I were both elderly when I returned to Cheju. In all the years I was gone, she never took off her wedding ring. My Korean wedding ring was long gone—I couldn't even tell you where it went.

Once we reconnected, every summer I would go to Cheju to be with In-sook and my son. This time with them became the highlight of my life.

In the years since the Korean War ended, the world changed. The taboo of cross-cultural marriages became more acceptable, but by this time, In-sook and I were too old to change our lives. Too many years had passed. When I was young, I thought that love would grow on trees and provide me one abundant harvest after another. I was naive and arrogant. It turned out that there was only one tree that provided me an abundant harvest. Only one tree that I would reach up to, marvel at its abundant beauty, its tenacity and strength, and its capacity to bloom year after year.

My son, Sang-ho, grew up to be more than I could've ever hoped or prayed for. He was a gifted architect, some would even say famous. He married late in life, no doubt a ramification of an absent father.

I watch my daughter, Emma, on Cheju. In particular, I watch her feet. I watch her step off of the jet bridge onto the land, and I watch her walk to the car. I watch her faint and need to be carried. I watch her move across the wooden floor of Min-sook's home and find her bearings enough to hike up Songsan, the extinct volcano.

I am struck by our feet and where they take us, how they literally carry us through our lives. When Emma stepped onto Cheju, I thought of the famous quote by astronaut Neil Armstrong, "One giant leap for mankind." In this case, it is one giant leap for the lineage of my family, and until this moment, it had been as far away as the moon .

In-sook Lee

It is true; Randall returned to me. All of the prayers, pleading, and bargaining with the gods finally brought him back. But by the time he returned to Cheju, we were old. The young blossoms of youthful love were replaced by the hues of a fading sunset.

Now the fate and destiny of this family is held in the hands of Emma, Randall's daughter. The two little girls, like perfect starfish, have washed upon the shore.

Of course, she will take them. Of course, she will take them into her hands, breathe them in, and be captivated by their delicate beauty. How could she not? So unexpected. Of course, Emma will see the miracle of it all. The greatest gift that her father and I can give her is to expand her own heart—to love in ways that she didn't know she could.

Sun-ja and Mi-ja are Emma's destiny and Parker's too. Like a tree whose roots expand and entwine with another's, our roots have grown together, unknown even to us, connecting us from one generation to another, across the world.

The Ancestors

Steam rises from the teacups. Parker and Emma sit on the front porch of the guesthouse. Parker holds the tour book in his hands. They are relaxing after the full morning of hiking. It is late afternoon; a gentle rain falls. Due to the rain, the falcon has been moved to the porch to be with them. It perches in the corner, eavesdropping.

Emma speaks to Parker but is looking at the falcon. "Isn't it interesting that Sang-ho brought a wounded wild bird here? I feel validated by my brother, like it's an affirmation. I can't quite put it into words, but it's about honoring the wounded."

Parker is listening, but he's distracted. "Emma, at some point, we need to talk about the elephant in the room."

"Well, we have successfully avoided that conversation until now." She takes a deep long breath. "The falcon and the elephant: the visible and the invisible. Which elephant? We're living with a herd. We could talk about my father having two wives at the same time and having a separate life here. This now explains his annual two-week fishing trip—alone—to Lake of the Woods. We could talk about a brother I had for my whole life and never knew. And, I might add, is now dead, and I will never know him. Or the grand finale, we could talk about two little girls who are now parentless."

"The two little girls."

"I don't know what to say."

"You must have some opinions."

"To be honest, I've been working hard just to breathe. I'm trying hard not to have an opinion, because I'm afraid I will start hyperventilating. What do you think?"

"This is your family, Emma. I think you need to be happy with what we decide, and it needs to be a decision we both can live with."

They drink their tea with unspoken words. Meanwhile, the rain falls and the falcon listens to their silence.

It is early morning and a gentle rain patters against the roof. Min-sook quietly peeks in the window of the guesthouse. Parker and Emma are asleep on the futon. Between them sleeps little Mi-ja. Min-sook quietly departs.

The sky grows brighter. A beautiful warm light begins to fill the tiny space. Parker moves in his sleep, his back to Mi-ja. His stirring wakes her up. Mi-ja is fascinated by Parker's hair. Her little fingers reinforce the waves, like a skilled hand sculpting Betty Crocker frosting.

Emma opens her eyes and is surprised to see Mi-ja in bed with them. Emma watches Mi-ja. Satisfied, Mi-ja crawls out of bed, not making a peep. Emma plays possum. At the foot of the bed, in her sweet little pajamas, Mi-ja bows to Emma and Parker and then tiptoes out of the guesthouse.

◆

Departure day has arrived. Emma and Parker's luggage sits waiting outside. The stress is evident on Emma's face. Min-sook is gracious and kind. She has packed food for them to take on the trip. Despite this circumstance, Min-sook is completely relaxed and even happy. Parker is reviewing the tickets and checking the passports. Mi-ja and Sun-ja are wearing their best dresses, the same clothes they welcomed Emma and Parker in. Emma has the digital camera and is taking photos. The two girls delightfully pose for the photographs.

Outside, two car doors slam. Mi-hee and Du-na walk toward the house. Mi-hee taps on the front door. "Hello!" she calls through the screen.

Sun-ja opens the front door and invites Mi-hee and Du-na in. Parker and Emma are organized and ready. There is happy conversation in Korean. Min-sook gives Emma a bag with food in it. Emma bows to Min-sook. Min-sook bows back. Emma steps forward and gives Min-sook a kiss on the cheek, and Min-sook smiles. Parker follows suit, and bows. The two little girls stand silently, watching the exit.

Emma turns to Sun-ja. "I'll write you, and you can read the letter to your sister and Auntie. How will that be?"

Sun-ja silently nods her head. Mi-ja's small face is full of sorrow and loss . Emma sees this and goes down on her knees. The tears begin to well in Mi-ja's eyes. A tear rolls down Mi-ja's cheek. Emma reaches up to catch it and puts it under her own eye. This makes Mi-ja smile. Emma puts her arms around Mi-ja and kisses her cheeks. She

261

then turns and hugs Sun-ja. Parker hugs Sun-ja and then Mi-ja.

With the mood getting emotional, Parker picks up the remaining carry-on luggage. "We'd better go, Emma," he says.

All of them exit the house and walk toward the car. The snake silently watches from the tree branches. At the car, Emma and Parker turn to Min-sook, Mi-ja, and Sun-ja.

Min-sook takes Emma's hands in her own and looks deep into her eyes, "한국 에 오기를 당 신을 감사하십시오. 나는 당신이소녀를 사랑할 것이라는 점을 알고 있다. 나는 그들이 당신의 생활 및 결혼에 축복일 것이라는 점을알고 있다. 것은 운명의 배열 이다. 나는 둘 다를만나게 아주 행복하다. 안전한 여행."

Having no idea what she just said, Emma expresses her gratitude in practiced Korean, "당신을 아주 많이 감사하십시오."

The three bow to Emma and Parker. Emma and Parker bow back. The luggage finds its way back into the vehicle, and all four take their respective places in the car. Mi-hee starts the engine and proceeds to drive away. They all wave out the car window and yell their goodbyes. Min-sook, Mi-ja, and Sun-ja wave and call out in return.

The little car speeds through the rural area on the dirt road. A cloud of dust is left in their wake. The car wheels go 'round and 'round.

The car wheels turn 'round and 'round. Emma and Parker are in Seoul in the back of a taxi. Emma is wearing white: a white linen blouse, unbuttoned, a white sleeveless

T-shirt, and a white skirt. She looks fresh and crisp in the heat. By contrast, Parker is already breaking a sweat as he anxiously glances at his watch.

The taxi driver talks into the rearview mirror to Parker, "Road construction."

Parker turns to Emma. "I'm not sure we're going to make the flight."

"I think we will, honey. It'll be all right." The toll of it all begins to show on Emma's face.

The taxi comes to a complete stop on a jammed street. Parker gets out his cell phone and a piece of paper. He dials a number.

"Do you speak English?" There is a long pause. "Thank you." Parker talks into the cell phone looking out the window. "Yes, this is Parker Carter. My wife and I have reservations on Korean Air flight 5168. We are stuck in traffic but on our way. Is that flight on time?"

There is another long pause.

"Thank you. Thank you very much." Parker ends the call.

He turns to Emma. "The flight is thirty minutes late. They have noted that we are on our way and will try to hold it for us."

The taxi driver seizes an opportunity and cuts through the traffic. He begins to drive through small streets like a race car on a racetrack. At last, he enters the airport and joins the congestion of even more cars, buses, and honking horns. Parker quickly gets money out of his wallet. The driver pulls over to the curb. All three jump out of the taxi. The taxi driver helps with the luggage.

"Hope you get plane," says the driver.

263

Parker hands him a number of Korean bills. The driver accepts the money with gratitude, bowing.

"Thank you very much." Parker quickly bows in return.

Emma and Parker run into the airport with a focused urgency, and people step out of their way. They search the terminal for the Korean Air sign. At the check-in counter, the attendant is talking on the phone. She looks up and sees them running through the crowd and aggressively waves for them to come to the head of the line. She speaks into the phone, giving information to someone, puts the phone down, and then loudly gives instructions in Korean for the passengers to stand aside and make room for the running Americans.

Emma and Parker arrive to the counter out of breath.

"Parker and Emma Carter?" the assistant asks.

"Yes!" says Parker as he hands her their passports and tickets.

She confirms all the information. Their bags are quickly checked at the counter.

"They're expecting you at the gate. You'll need to run. Go to the front of the security line. The gate is the last one down the corridor, Gate 18. We will hold the plane for you."

They run to the front of security; people step out of their way. They are checked through. The corridor is long and appears to curve with the Earth. They seem to be moving in slow motion. Emma desperately tries to manage her tapestry carry-on. Her white skirt floats behind her. Korean faces turn to watch them run past. Emma is not only running for the plane but also running from Korea,

264

the children, and their unmet needs. She is fleeing the country, like her father did, fifty years earlier.

In the distance, at Gate 18, the attendant waves at Emma and Parker. The sprint continues. Out of breath, they arrive at the gate and quickly hand over their boarding passes. The airport personnel holds the boarding door open for them to run through. Emma and Parker gasp for air while the stewardess greets them calmly.

The airplane door closes behind them. The plane is full of older Koreans. Most have a name tag pinned on the upper left-hand side of their clothing, as if they are all on some sort of organized tour. Everyone appears relaxed and ready for departure. Emma and Parker take their seats in the front row in coach class. They have aisle seats across from each other. There is an old man already sleeping next to Parker. A large, heavy Korean woman sits next to Emma. Emma and Parker look and feel as though they just ran the New York Marathon; the only things missing are their vests with numbers.

Emma struggles for air. "Oh my god, I never want to do that again!"

"We barely made it!" Parker says as he wipes the sweat off his face and neck.

Emma begins to laugh, relief taking hold. "We made it!"

She leans against the seat, closes her eyes, and tries to calm her breathing. The stewardess speaks in Korean to the large woman seated next to Emma. Their talking interrupts Emma's attempted meditation. There seems to be some negotiation going on and some gesturing toward Emma. Emma doesn't care. She is out of here, going home. The plane backs up and proceeds to the runway while the safety announcements are made.

The engine goes into full gear, picking up speed as it taxies down the runway. The wheels turn 'round and 'round, lift off the ground, and fold under the plane. The plane begins to soar across the expansive blue sky. With a comfortable altitude attained, the Korean stewardess returns. Emma's seat-mate gathers her things, gently bows to Emma and leaves, escorted by the stewardess.

Parker looks at Emma. "I'll give you $10 to switch seats with me."

"No way." She gives him a wink and a smile.

The empty seat isn't vacant for long. The stewardess returns and holds the hand of a little girl who is around six years old. The child is a fawn in headlights. A ribbon with a name tag hangs around her neck. It reads: "My name is Jeong-mi Kang. I'm going to New York City. Kathy and Steve Maryhart will meet me." The stewardess gets the child settled into the seat and fastens her belt.

The stewardess turns to Emma and speaks in perfect English, "She was toward the back of the plane, next to teenage boys. I thought she would be more comfortable up here next to you. I didn't think you'd mind."

Emma hesitates. "That's fine."

"Thank you," says the stewardess. She then turns to the child, "그녀는 사랑스러운 숙녀와 같이 보인다. 당신은 그녀의 옆에 안락할 것이다."

Jeong-mi looks up at Emma, then nods in agreement to the stewardess. The child is quiet and demure. The stewardess smiles and returns to her duties.

266

Emma looks over to Parker. She should have accepted the $10 offer. No words are exchanged. Emma closes her eyes. Within moments, Jeong-mi is touching Emma's hair, feeling it, just like Mi-ja did. Emma turns to look at her. Their eyes meet and lock. Each has a story to tell, each has a history, and each has heartache.

Emma has not escaped. Profound and deep emotions overwhelm her. She begins to cry the tears of generations. Emma's emotional damn has burst wide open, and there is no stopping the flood. Parker reaches over and tries to console his wife. The sound of sobbing spreads through the airplane cabin like wildfire. Anxiety and stress begin to rise in the passengers.

The stewardess comes quickly to see what the commotion is. "What is wrong? Please, you must get a hold of yourself."

Emma tries unsuccessfully to stop crying.

The stewardess turns to Parker. "She is upsetting the passengers. What's wrong?"

"It's a family situation."

The stewardess begins to sound desperate. "Please sir, you must help your wife gain control."

Parker grasps Emma's arm. "Get up. Let's go to the bathroom."

In front of 150 concerned passengers, Emma and Parker go into the bathroom built for one. Parker struggles to shut the door.

Emma and Parker face each other, flying above the earth—suspended—in a two-foot space, complete with air-sucking toilet. Emma's face is streaked with tears, her hair matted to her cheeks. She tries to breathe, her hand held to her chest.

267

"Emma, it's not our responsibility."

"Then who?! Who is responsible?!" A demanding hysteria has crept into Emma's voice.

The passengers are listening, trying to figure out what is wrong with the Americans. They can hear speaking but most don't know the language. An older Korean woman stands up and addresses the passengers in Korean, "영어를 누구가 말하는지."

A silence spreads throughout the cabin. Once again she demands, "영어를 누구가 말하는지."

An elderly man stands up, close to the bathroom. He speaks with deep compassion, "그는 그들의 책임이 아니다는 것을 말한다. 그 때 책임있는 그녀는 묻는가? He says it is not their responsibility. She asks, 'Who is responsible?'"

This is better than any airplane movie. The old man moves to the aisle and leans on his wooden cane, facing his captivated audience. All faces look to the interpreter. They anxiously wait for the next installment of dialogue.

Emma sobs. "When does it end? Generation after generation we look away, and every generation pays a price. My father looked away and now I'm looking away, too." She pauses to take a breath. "It's clear: I am my father's daughter."

The elderly man looks over his captivated audience and pauses before speaking, "누구가 우리의 조상의 부상에 책임 있는가?그녀의 아버지는 그의 운명을 사절했다. 그녀는 그녀의 것을 사절하는 것을 시도하고 있다. 그녀는 그녀의아버지 같이 다만 이다. Who is responsible for the wounds of our ancestors? Her father refused his destiny. She is trying to refuse hers. She is just like her father."

Sadness spreads over the passengers. Kleenex tissues come out, eyes are dabbed.

"그녀는 그녀의 아버지의 특성의 부상을 나른다. She carries the wound of her father's character."

Emma is now yelling, "What is your plan, that we mail them money? They don't need money—they need a home and to be loved. That's just what my father did to appease his guilt. 'The check is in the mail.' " There is a momentary pause. "Everything—always—was in the mail. 'I'm sending you love.' Well guess what: the love never arrived ."

The interpreter, now center stage, is the embodiment of ancient wisdom. "심장은 어떻게 그 것이 사랑하는 것은 준비되어 있는 언제 지 아는가? 진실하고 그리고 순수하다 경우, 그것이 모든 국경을 넘어갈, 모든 시간을 초월하고, 넋의 갈망을 치유한다. 그녀는 그에, 출석해, 순간에서 살고 그리고 결석한 제스처를 만들지 않기 위하여 그를 위한 책임을인정하는 도전한다." How does the heart know when it is ready to love? When true and pure, it crosses all borders, transcends all time, and heals the longing of the soul. She challenges him to be present, to live in the moment and accept responsibility for that, not make absent gestures."

Parker is exhausted. "Emma, we aren't going to solve this here in the bathroom. We're both tired, and this trip has been overwhelming. Let's go back and sit down. For right now, let's focus on getting home. And god forbid, that little girl sitting next to you thinks she's done something wrong."

Emma looks a mess. Parker puts his arms around her and kisses her.

The elderly man, full of grace, speaks slowly with compassion. "시즌 같이, 이것에는 너 무 그것이 시간을 소유하기위한 것이다 있다. 우리는 봄의 자두 꽃송이를 돌진할 수 없다, 도 아니다 우 리는 강제한다 그것의호박색 숄을 착용하기 위하여 단풍나무를 할 수 있다. 일단은, 우리는 집으로 가고 펼치기 위하여 운명을 기다린다. Like the seasons, this too has its own time. We cannot rush the plum blossoms of spring, nor can we force the maple tree to wear its amber shawl. For now, we go home and wait for destiny to unfold."

Emma surrenders. "All right."

Parker turns around in the small space and struggles to open the door. They exit one after the other.

The wise old man remains standing. He faces the returning Emma and Parker and bows with honor toward them. All of the faces in the cabin look at them. Some continue to dab their eyes. It is clear, despite cultural differences, the stories are the same, relatable, and understood. Emma and Parker, sensing they have just been the main focus of the entire cabin, sit down. Emma quickly fastens her seat belt in an effort to stabilize her own internal turbulence.

Emma turns off the Jeep and unfastens her seat belt. She gets out of the car, opens up the trunk, and grabs various department store bags: Target, The Gap, and Shoe Town. She opens the front door to the house. Parker is sitting on the couch reading the newspaper.

"Hi, honey!" Emma sounds exceedingly happy.

"Looks like you were successful! What'd you buy?"

"Well, I got underwear for the girls, some darling jeans, a couple of jackets from Target, two toys, and some shoes. I bought Min-sook a nightgown." It is clear that Emma is quite pleased with herself, and this makes Parker happy too.

Emma goes to her office and puts the bags down on the guest bed. There is an empty shipping box waiting to be filled. Her computer reveals her updated "wallpaper," a photograph taken of the girls in their festive dresses. Emma proceeds to take the gifts out of the bags. There is a parade of purchases. She admires them all as she removes the price tags. The items are carefully placed in the box. One side of the box is for Sun-ja, the other for Mi-ja.

Last, but certainly not least, are the two shoe boxes. Emma carefully takes a shoe box, as though it's sacred, and lifts the lid. She unfolds the tissue to reveal a pair of red sequined shoes. She lifts the shoes out of the box and holds them up into the light. Brilliant, glimmering light dances upon sequins—Dorothy's ruby slippers. She admires their beauty and then sets them in the shipping box. She opens the second sacred shoe box and parts the white tissue to reveal another smaller pair of ruby red slippers. She puts them in the shipping box. The two pairs sit side by side.

Parker walks into the room with a cup of tea for Emma. Argos is at his side. Argos looks at a framed photo of the girls and begins to bark with his tail wagging in excitement. Emma reaches down to him, taking his muzzle in her hands. "What's up with you?" She proceeds to give him a kiss smack dab on the middle of his head.

"I brought you some tea," Parker says, as he stands holding the cup and saucer, the one with the Korean woman embedded in the porcelain. He surveys the bed with the fanfare of gifts: bags, tissue, and tags are everywhere. Parker proceeds to take a sip of tea from Emma's cup.

Emma watches Parker drink from her cup, appreciating the unconscious significance of the gesture. "Thank you honey," she says to him, her eyes twinkling.

Parker looks into the box and sees two pairs of ruby slippers sitting side by side.

He starts to laugh. "Emma, you bought them ruby slippers?"

"Yes, I did."

"Those aren't very practical," he says, with a tone that is both entertained but questioning.

Emma pauses. She lifts a pair of ruby slippers out of the box and holds them in both hands as though they are sacred. Ever so gently she turns them in the light so that the sequins glisten.

She smiles at her husband, "Well, it all depends."

A Korean Air flight departing from Seoul slowly moves down the tarmac to ready its position for takeoff. The passengers rearrange themselves, position pillows, speak in quiet voices and organize their reading materials. They are settling in for the long flight to the United States. The same stewardess from Emma and Parker's trip demonstrates the use of the safety belt. Her eyes glance over the passengers. She smiles as she makes eye contact with a few of them. Speaking in Korean, the stewardess gestures to the exit doors, points to the seat lights along the floor, and then holds the breathing mask to her own face. She turns her face to the side, which shows her profile, the mask securely in place.

The stewardess looks over to the two little girls who sit in the front row: Sun-ja and Mi-ja each wear their obligatory nametags that dangle around their necks. The girls are laughing and captivated by something. The stewardess takes a step forward to get a better view of what has their attention. They are looking at their shoes. They pivot their toes and admire the light reflected in the sequins and brilliant red of their matching ruby slippers. Prisms of color begin to dance all over the inside of the plane. Laughing, Min-ja reaches out and tries to capture a moving rainbow.

"I believe there is within each one of us—perhaps in our
DNA—the ability to make the world a better place.
We have that opportunity in small ways on a daily basis.
Other times, perhaps our ideas are larger, grander,
and a bit more challenging. If instead of actualizing
our potential, we succumb to complacency,
isn't that—in its own way—a crime against humanity?"

Edie Barrett

Suggested Reading

For me, artistic expression, social and ecological
responsibility, spirituality, and Jungian psychology are
deeply intertwined. All have been essential components
to my development and my continuing evolution. My
creative expression is multidimensional. My life is also
multidimensional. The following are resources that have
been meaningful to my growth. Perhaps you will find them
meaningful as well.

Stephen Aizenstat. *Dream Tending.*
 The sacredness and honoring of the dream world
is palpable in Stephen Aizenstat's work. His writing is
very poetic and lyrical, and in this regard, embodies the
landscape of dream. I consider this book to be a major
contribution to the field of dream interpretation.

Brené Brown. *Daring Greatly.*
 I'm part of a dream group. We used Brené Brown's

Daring Greatly for nearly two years as a backdrop for our time together. Brown is a research professor (which means her work is grounded in research versus her own theories) from Houston, Texas. If you are not already familiar with her work, I would recommend watching one of her TED talks on intimacy and vulnerability. She is not a Jungian, but her concepts are foundational in terms of self-understanding.

James Hillman. *The Soul's Code.*
James Hillman was a major contributor to post-Jungian thought.

Robert A. Johnson. *Balancing Heaven and Earth.*
Robert A. Johnson is a second-generation Jungian from Zürich, Switzerland. He offers a fabulous and accessible introduction to the world of Jungian psychology. I have found his work to be tremendously validating in regard to understanding my own process. This is a great book to start with!

Carl Jung. *Memories, Dreams, Reflections.*
Carl Jung's autobiography, *Memories, Dreams, Reflections*, tracks the psychological journey of individuation. On a deep level he acquiesces to a creative archetypal force. His experience is at times psychologically dangerous, and yet he acknowledges this surrender was the most fruitful period of his work. I believe this book is essential reading for anyone who embarks on his or her own process of individuation. I define this book as fairly advanced and would suggest you read the other books first.

Thomas Moore. *Care of the Soul: How to Add Depth and Meaning to Your Everyday Life.*
I would recommend the illustrated edition, which has a copyright date of 1998. This is a beautiful book. He does a stunning job weaving art, mythology, and Jungian psychology all together through a therapist's lens.

Some insightful, meaningful passages in Moore's book include:

"The intellect wants to know; the soul likes to be surprised. Intellect, looking outward, wants enlightenment and the pleasure of a burning enthusiasm. The soul, always drawn inward, seeks contemplation and the more shadowy, mysterious experience of the underworld."

"Often, when spirituality loses its soul, it takes on the shadow-form of fundamentalism."

"The soul apparently needs amorous sadness. It is a form of consciousness that brings its own unique wisdom."

"It has often been noted that most, if not all, problems brought to therapists are issues of love. It makes sense then that the cure is also love."

Carol Pearson. *The Hero Within: Six Archetypes We Live By.* 3rd ed., 1998.
I would recommend this specific edition. This book is valuable for someone who wants to understand what archetypes mean and how to apply them to our lives. She explores six archetypes. If you're interested in creative self-exploration, I would highly recommend this book.

Dennis Slattery. *A Pilgrimage Beyond Belief: Spiritual Journeys through Christian and Buddhist Monasteries of the American West.*

Dennis is a prolific writer, but this remains my favorite book of his. I enjoyed going on my own imaginary pilgrimage with him. Beautifully written.

Dennis Slattery. *Bridge Work: Essays on Mythology, Literature and Psychology.*

This book is skillfully and poetically articulated.

Richard Tarnas. *The Passion of the Western Mind.*

John E. Mack, a professor of psychiatry at Harvard Medical School, wrote this for Tarnas' book: "An extraordinary work of scholarship. It not only places the history of Western thought in perspective but derives new insights concerning the evolution of our thinking and the future of the whole human enterprise." I could not have said it better.

Suggested Listening

Krista Tippett's weekly radio show (podcast) *On Being* takes place each Sunday morning on MPR from 6 a.m. to 7 a.m. The show's website contains an archive of past interviews dating back to 2001. I'm not sure what I would do without her radio show. She is a link to world perspectives on spirituality, science, psychology, cultural and ecological awareness, and the arts.

These are a few of the episodes of her show that have been valuable to me and bridge conversations of poetry, art, spirituality, and landscape.

Ann Hamilton. "Making, and the Spaces We Share." November 19, 2015,

Once upon a time, when I was a UCSB student, I had an art class with Ann Hamilton. I don't remember much about the class, because it was an independent study of sculpture, but I remember being *fascinated* by her. She was so totally out of the box for me. Her work was—and continues to be—so original. So for a few reasons, I really love this interview. It is very difficult to talk about art, and I find Ann Hamilton speaks a language that I relate to. She uses phrases such as "embodied knowledge" and "cellular memory" and addresses topics such as "that in-between space when answers come at their own pace." She also talks about a creative process as being sacred and private and poses the interesting question: "How do we trust our process when we can't exactly name it?"

Pico Iyer. "The Art of Stillness." June 4, 2015,

Pico Iyer is a journalist and writer who is an avid world traveler. I have a soft spot for him in my heart because he was part of the University of California Santa Barbara Lecture Series. He often interviewed world luminaries, and I'm delighted that he is now the one being interviewed. He believes that the "greater adventure is the inner landscape." He believes that it is a conscious choice to be present and it is, in fact, a practice.

Yo-Yo Ma. "Music Happens between the Notes." March 3, 2016.

What a fantastic interview with world-renowned cellist Yo-Yo Ma! Krista Tippett asks him to define beauty. I'm slightly recapping this, "Beauty is transcendence—

most often in nature—when that encapsulated form is received, there is a moment of reception and cognition of the thing which is startling. . . . If we are part of nature and observe nature. . . . There is a transfer of life" (from the unedited interview, located at 1:27:18).

Mary Oliver. "Listening to the World." October 15, 2015,
 Of course, Mary Oliver is also part of this list. I treasure hearing her read her own poetry! Her work is profoundly influenced by nature, which is reflected in her work. I relate to her childhood of poverty and the reflection on nature being her companion and healer.

Lewis Newman. "The Refreshing Practice of Repentance." September 17, 2015,
 Lewis Newman is a St. Paul, Minnesota, resident and the associate dean of Carleton College. Although he has a focus on Jewish traditions, the concepts are applicable to all of us.
 My takeaway from the Newman interview: to embrace our creativity—regardless of its expression—I think it's imperative that we make peace with the wounds of our personal history so that we don't diminish our creative potential. At a minimum, if we cannot be at peace with our past, then I think it's important to find a way to embrace conscious awareness so that we can do the creative work we are meant to do and fully embrace what it means to be alive and participate in the goodness of the world.

Jewish Rabbi Lawrence Kushner. "Kabbalah and the Inner Life of God." March 10, 2016,

It's interesting to me that this is my second Jewish entry. I have no experience with Jewish traditions. However, this, for me, is an illustration of the value of being open to another perspective. I relate to this more than I could've ever imagined. The value of exposing ourselves to other philosophies and world religions is that sometimes we can see ourselves through another's lens, and in doing so, we find a commonality of what connects us versus what divides us.

Quotes from Rabbi Lawrence Kushner:

"Old-time religion wants to know what God wants us to do, whereas a mystical variety of the same spiritual tradition would say, no, I want to know what God knows. I want to see the world through God's eyes. I want to lose myself in the divine all. That's how I want to make sense out of religion" (edited interview, located at 34:19).

Kushner talks about the work of William James and his definition of mysticism (edited interview at 13:16):

1. That it's transient. The experience comes and goes on its own accord and on its own timetable. It is not something that I can manifest myself.
2. That I am passive. I don't have the experience; it has me.
3. Noetic equals there is an intellectual content to it, but...
4. I am not able to put the experience into words."

Kushner defines a mystical experience is *intensely personal.*

Suggested Viewing

Joseph Campbell. *The Power of Myth with Bill Moyers.*
I watch this series at least once a year. It reminds me of my place in the long line of humanity, which is both humbling and inspiring.

Gregory Cobert. *Ashes to Snow.*
This film leaves me speechless every time I watch it. I am deeply grateful I was able to see this exhibit when it was in Los Angeles.

Marie-Louise von Franz, with an introduction from Marion Woodman. *The Way of the Dream.*
I received this video set as a gift from Marion Woodman. Consequently, for many reasons I appreciate it. I absolutely love seeing Marion! I have a deep respect for the work of Marie-Louise von Franz and it is very intriguing to watch her talk about dreams.

Andy Goldsworthy. *Rivers and Tides.*
Just beautiful! I love his work and feel a kinship with his engagement with nature.

Robert A. Johnson. *Slender Threads: A Conversation with Robert A. Johnson.*
Being a big Robert Johnson fan, I treasure this interview.

TED Talks

I hope that you will find these resources inspirational for your own work:

Brené Brown. "Listening to Shame." March 2012, https://www.ted.com/talks/brene_brown_listening_to_shame/. Pico Iyer. "The Art of Stillness." August 2014, https://www.ted.com/talks/pico_iyer_the_art_of_stillness.

Shonda Rhimes. "My Year of Saying Yes to Everything." February 2016, https://www.ted.com/talks/shonda_rhimes_my_year_of_saying_yes_to_everything.

"We are not human beings having a spiritual experience. We are spiritual beings having a human experience."

Pierre Teilhard de Chardin (1881–1955)
French philosopher and Jesuit priest

About the Author

Edie Barrett is a fifth generation Minnesota Norwegian. She is a lifelong artist, poet and writer. She returned to Minnesota in 2010, after living in Santa Barbara, California, for twenty-six years.

As a fine artist and poet, her work seeks to honor and celebrate rural lifestyle.

In 2018, she was accepted into the graduate program of Humphrey School of Public Affairs at the University of Minnesota. She will be pursuing a Master's Degree in Public Affairs. It is her hope to use art as the vehicle for social engagement and change.

Edie resides in Ortonville, Minnesota, with Lizzie, the Yorkshire Terrier, and Max and Mimi, the two feral kittens that arrived at the back door.

She is grateful for the inspirational beauty of her life on the prairie.

For further information, please visit her website:
ediebarrett.com